Honeymoon with Death

Honeymoon with Death

and other stories

Bridget Penney

Polygon
EDINBURGH

© Bridget Penney, 1991

First published 1991 by
Polygon, 22 George Square, Edinburgh

Set in Sabon by Koinonia, Bury and
printed and bound in Great Britain
by Redwood Press, Melksham, Wiltshire

British Library Cataloguing in Publication Data
Penney, Bridget
Honeymoon with death.
  I. Title
  823.914 [F]

ISBN 0 7486 6102 6

The publisher acknowledges subsidy
from the Scottish Arts Council
towards the publication of this volume.

Contents

Honeymoon with Death   7

The Kitty and Jenny Gang   52

Incidents on the Road   75

Sister Anne   90

The Girlfriend   108

Spike and Scissors   121

Goldtown   142

His Right Hand   152

Honeymoon with Death

Lucy

Romance. She was afraid of the word, with its sickly connotations of orange trees and silvery moonlight. She remembered the long warm nights in Cyprus beneath the open sky, the road along the cliff above the sea, gardens carved out of the rock, and mimosa erratically perfuming the breeze. She remembered her early marriage which had turned sour so quickly she was left half-stunned by the elusive nature of what she'd only begun to grasp. She remembered the cold flight back to London, alone, when she swore with the fervour and passion of a youthful tragedy that it would never happen again.

She stuck to it. The memory was overlaid but not buried by five years of others. Her life ran smoothly into certain grooves. As time passed, she grew to despise herself a little. There was a certain fatalism in her nature she felt was cheap. She made herself narrow and scrupulous, turning her susceptibility into a weapon against herself.

She was assistant manager at the restaurant where she'd worked for three years. She supervised the other staff and dealt with all the cash. When they were busy at lunchtime she sat behind the till. That was how she first met him. He pushed his tray along the counter like anyone else, then gave her a handful of crumpled Scottish one pound notes. She looked up and said

– I'm afraid we can't accept these.

– Course you can.

He grinned at her. She stared round for the manager but could only see the queue of impatient, hungry people building up behind this man. So she shrugged and rang up the amount. Their hands touched as she gave him his change which he dropped rather ostentatiously in the staff box. Her eyes

7

flickered a slight but well-contained irritation. Then he smiled at her again, and took his tray to a table. As she rang up meal after meal, she was conscious of him watching her. Customers often did when they came in to eat alone and had nothing else to occupy them. But this one she didn't mind. She found herself stealing the odd glance at him, and once their eyes met, but with a sudden apprehension of panic she froze him out. When he went she felt unease at an abortive encounter which might have meant something more. When Mandy came to relieve her on the till, she smiled at her automatically, and for the rest of the afternoon was conscious of catching herself out from time to time, as she couldn't settle to any of her work.

But he came back the next day, and the next. She knew she smiled when she saw him.

– You're unadventurous, she said when, on the third day running, the items on his tray were the same.

– You don't change your dress either.

She looked down at herself automatically. The dress was a dark colour with white collar and cuffs.

– It suits you.

She smiled at him.

– Come and have coffee with me.

She glanced around. – Not here.

– Are you busy tonight?

– Working until ten.

– I'll pick you up then if you like.

She'd lowered her head, hardly daring to nod. Waiting for him on the dark street by the back entrance she was conscious only of being afraid that he wouldn't show up. He was ten minutes late. When she heard the hurrying footsteps, she drew back instinctively into the doorway.

He took her hand.

– I don't even know your name.

– I'm Nick.

They passed three pubs both rejected as being too full. Down a side street was a shadowy almost deserted wine bar. She let herself be led in there, they sat down. Nick ordered whisky. She hesitated then said she wanted crème de menthe.

8

When it came, a thick green syrup in its small glass, he took it from her gently a moment and sniffed it.

– I never met a man who liked to drink it, she said.

– Perhaps I'll be the first.

He tasted it and made a face. She laughed.

– You should believe me.

She thought she could still remember what he looked like at that moment years later.

– You're lonely.

– There's worse things than being lonely.

– Do you think so? he said softly. A funny little smile came round the corners of her mouth.

After that he stopped coming into the restaurant. Instead they spent hours in airless rooms where they stayed just long enough to make love. She had a confused memory of wallpapers and soft beds. The rest of her life grew increasingly remote. She worked with the same scrupulous precision, but it went to waste. A couple of times she caught Mandy looking at her as if she wanted to talk.

– What's the matter? she said one day when they were in the kitchen.

– Tony bothers me.

Lucy stared dreamily at the girl. – Do you want me to say something?

Mandy looked away, confused but shifty. – I can't afford to lose my job.

– You don't keep her up to scratch, said Tony, composed, in the office later.

– She doesn't work hard enough. That's all I said. That's what I meant.

– Mandy does all right, said Lucy.

He looked at her. – You need a holiday. I've been thinking of late you don't look yourself.

– I don't want... she began, then fell silent and nodded.

That night she put her hand up gently to Nick's chin, then traced his lips.

– How would you like to go away?

– I've been meaning to talk to you about that kind of thing.

9

– Oh?

She twined her legs round him. He rolled sideways so that she came over on top of him.

– Our future.

– That sounds so grand.

– His face changed. She could see it even in the dim light. Still smiling, she said

– What's the matter?

– Oh this. This room; cheap, damp, and shoddy. This way of life.

Her smile died. She laid her head on his chest.

– You know how it is when you haven't got any money.

She raised her head. – What does that kind of thing matter? I love you.

– That's why I want something a bit better. For us. Money only matters when you haven't got enough.

He pulled himself upright against the pillows, put a hand on her hair.

– You can't pretend you like living like this.

– I hadn't really thought about it, she said, but of course she had. – I just thought we'd go on as we are, she ended lamely, seeing his dissatisfaction.

– Don't you want to be with me, Lucy?

– Why do you think I'm here.

– Say in a year's time, even a month. Do you want to get old like this?

She was silent.

– You don't want to deal on those terms, he said softly. – As far as you're concerned I'm just a casual pick up. Tell me. I can stand it.

– I can't, she said with her face in the pillow. She felt his hand on her back, tracing the contour of her spine.

– I have to go away.

– You're leaving London? You want to?

She rolled over.

– Whether I want to or not isn't exactly the issue.

She watched him.

– Is anything the matter?

He put his hand up to her mouth.

– It doesn't have to be.

As she stared at him her eyes registered comprehension. She looked away a moment, then back.

– Don't tell me you've never thought of it.

– I've thought of it all right, she said slowly. – Everyone thinks of things like that. But the difference lies between thinking and doing it.

She got out of bed abruptly. Her tights laddered as she pulled them on too quickly. She swore, looked up, and caught him looking at her in the dressing-table mirror.

– Will I see you again?

– Next week. Give me a week, she said. – I'll meet you, she scribbled an address she knew. – If I'm not there you'll know I've decided not to.

He took the paper reluctantly but she noticed him fold it away with care. – So perhaps this is goodbye.

She had to kiss him. When at last they pulled apart she said

– Nick!

and felt his arms round her again. – Tomorrow, she whispered. – It's Friday and Tony has the books from his other businesses brought along so he can check all the takings before they're banked. He puts the money in his safe, till late. Then I go to the bank.

– Why doesn't he leave it in his own safe.

– He doesn't trust it when he's not there. Silly, she muttered half forgetting.

He was filling her ears with what he would do.

– Nick, she said uneasily, breaking away – you know I wouldn't do this if I didn't love you.

Staring at her troubled face he said – You're a special girl, Lucy. Special to me. I thought so the first time I saw you.

The bag felt heavy as she walked along. It was tucked inside a shoulder bag that any woman might carry, but it was secured with a leather strap she wound nervously about her wrist. She'd never minded carrying the money before: it was only a short distance to the bank, half the length of the street, a left

11

turn, then another hundred yards. She trod between the pools of light cast by the street lamps, seeming to avoid them as if she was afraid of the light catching her face, and what it might show. She'd tried to cover her pallor with make-up, but somehow it made it more pronounced, and the dark shadows under her eyes made them look much bigger. She was reasoning with herself as she walked along – it's only paper, it's covered by insurance, it won't make any difference to them. And a self-justifying anger to bolster it up – how can they expect loyalty, isn't it time I had something for myself? Compared to the amounts you read about every day in the paper changing hands, it's nothing, but it's enough to give us a chance of happiness.

For a moment she stood still, agonisingly aware of her own suspicions. She whispered to herself – He can't have thought that.

– Then why did he say about the money?

– That's how he is. He can't help it.

– I love him. I'm a fool. What am I doing?

She walked a little further, then paused again at the intersection where she could turn off for the bank. She stared into the darkness on her left, where she could dimly make out the shape of its illuminated sign. Her feet shuffled, then stopped. The leather strap pulled tighter round her hand so it dug into her flesh. She thought

– If I go now, I step right out of the pattern of my life.

Her feelings were mixed: a sense of panic at the prospect presented and also of excitement. A revulsion at the way her life had gone and the stagnation of the last five years. The thought occurred to her that she could put the money in the night safe and go to Nick empty-handed. It would be the way to set all her doubts at rest, and yet she wouldn't allow herself to take it. She couldn't face the thought of rejection.

Or she could pay the money in, go home, forget him, settle down in the same slowly progressive pattern and be safe. But she didn't want to be safe. Finally her head turned and she went right, crossing the road with steps that seemed too deliberate in their purpose, walking swiftly along the next street, even running as she neared the far end to give herself less time to think over what she was doing.

He was waiting in a little car.

– You've got it? Good.

She heard her own voice, apparently detached.

– We should be clear till Monday. That branch isn't open tomorrow so he won't have a chance to check it.

– We'd better get away from here.

With an uncertain pang she noticed how nervous he sounded. She kept silent, still, pulling down the passenger shade to shield her face from him a little, quickly adjusting the angle to banish her reflection from the mirror.

Nick

They headed south by a circuitous route, driving fifty miles up the M1 before turning off to weave their way slowly back through small towns and side roads. They stopped a couple of times to fill up the car and eat. Lucy remembered pushing bacon and eggs round her plate with a fork, while Nick sipped his coffee across from her, apparently sunk in a private gloom.

On Saturday afternoon they pulled up in a lonely lane in mid-Sussex. Lucy let the engine die for a minute and they sat quietly, staring at the overgrown hedges thick with ripening fruit.

– There's something just up ahead, Nick, she said. – I'm too tired to drive any more.

He could just see the roof of what looked like a barn through a gap in the hedge. They changed places. She put her head on his shoulder, then he started the car and they drove slowly up the rutted private road.

It looked like a dealer's yard, seeming incongruous to them in the middle of the country. Set well back from the road was a high fence enclosing the broken bodies of cars stacked high. As they progressed cautiously up the track, a couple of dogs rushed out, barking wildly.

– Nick, look!

As they rounded a bend she saw a row of caravans parked

beyond the wire. They looked gleaming white and new. She reckoned that they were jammed too close together for anyone to be staying there.

– If we had one, we could get some sleep, she said quickly. – We could hide out in the forest for a while, where no one would find us.

He was quiet for a while, then nodded.

– All right, he said and this time his voice was tired.

They stopped outside the house. The shape of the original cottage, which had been extended, still showed. It was in bad repair. Round the back were farm buildings, dominated by the open barn they'd noticed from the road.

– Well, said Nick – they're obviously not farmers.

The two dogs jumped up against the side of the car, scrabbling. Nick pressed the horn with the flat of his hand. After a few minutes, a thick-set man emerged from round the side of the house.

– Let me talk to him.

He wound down the window as the man approached, calling off his dogs.

–You're on a private road.

– We know.

Nick got out of the car, slamming the door. He and the man moved away a little so Lucy couldn't quite hear what they were saying. She rested her head on the seat and closed her eyes. Then she heard steps approaching the car and jerked upright again.

– Cash, have you? the other man was saying.

– Lucy, said Nick.

Her eyes met his, didn't trouble to conceal her anger. Then she stared at the other man, who turned slightly as if shy of being looked at.

Nick slid back into the seat beside her as the man went into the house.

– What did you tell him for? You idiot, you don't know who these people are. We'd better get out of here now. Did you see the way he was looking at us?

He gripped her wrist. – Get the money out, Lucy.

14

She was still, so he reached across her and drew the satchel out himself.

– The caravans aren't for sale on any other terms.

– Then they're stolen.

– Of course they are. But that's better for us, if they're untraceable.

She was silent.

– You can go back to London right now and put the money back in that safe.

– No, she said quietly.

– Then. don't be so fussy.

He let go of her wrist.

– They're coming back, she said quickly.

This time they both got out of the car. Lucy squinted against the late afternoon sun that just caught over the roofs. The thick-set man seemed dwarfed by his companion, who was a thin but powerful-looking man in a grey suit that flapped about him. He shook Nick's hand, seeming barely to glance at Lucy.

– I'm Flanagan.

Somehow he reminded her of a hawk. The thick-set man brought up the rear. Lucy stepped across the muddy cracks in her light shoes.

– So you're on your honeymoon, Mrs Scott, said Flanagan, looking round.

There was something about his eyes that she disliked. They had that trick of never seeming to leave her, yet whenever she looked up, she couldn't have said that he was actually staring at her.

– Yes.

He unlocked the caravans, one after another to show them the interiors, but never said anything more and the thick-set man was also completely silent. Lucy tried to contain her unease and chatted to Nick in a rather strained way. Gradually, as they made their way along the line, they stopped talking.

– This one, said Nick at last.

Flanagan watched them from the step.

– How much?

Flanagan turned to the thick-set man who glanced up and swallowed.

– A thousand.

– Cheap, said Nick. He held the canvas bag.

– Gas cylinder's full, said the thick-set man. He looked over to his companion again. – Everything's included.

Flanagan was looking away. Lucy watched Nick's hands fumble with the bag, trying to count off the notes without revealing how much was inside. He handed them to the thick-set man.

– Looks like they won the pools, George, Flanagan said.

An uneasy smile played across Nick's face.

– Races. Accumulator.

– You're a lucky man.

Flanagan smiled. – Why not give me a tip? What was the last horse you won on?

Nick said quietly, – Wedding Bells. In the 3.30 at Doncaster. We figured it couldn't lose.

Flanagan laughed.

– It's enough of a gamble getting married. Isn't it, Mrs Scott?

She felt it as a threat, looked up with a flash of uneasy panic.

– I hope it works out for you both, he continued. – If you're looking for a place to park, a friend of mine has a little site up in the forest. Just near a farm where you can get some food. If Mrs Scott likes the country, that is. Tell him I sent you.

– He's got a woman there.

Nick glanced in the side mirror as they pulled out of the yard.

– Where?

– She's gone back in the house. Big woman. Lucy, he said gently, after a while. – Everything'll be fine now, you'll see.

She smiled, and put her arm tentatively across the back of his seat.

– We'll end up off the road, he said, his eyes on the mirror.

– So what? I'd be with you. At least nothing more could go wrong.

– Cheerful today, aren't you?

She didn't reply.

The road wound up into the forest. They passed a cluster of houses set back from the road, a garage, a pub, and that was all. Gradually the trees took over. They pulled off the main road up a track. The car's suspension bumped and they could see the caravan swaying all over the place. Nick drove steadily, trying to avoid the potholes. At last he switched the engine off and they just sat.

– Here?

– You didn't want to go to that place he said about.

She shook her head. They got out of the car, stood still and listened. She wasn't conscious of a breeze, but they could see it at work among the trees, lifting branches, gently tossing, murmuring. She felt there was something magical about the place. It was still and dim among the trees; as she walked around she saw they were mostly conifers, with a few old patches of oaks that had been there before.

Nick touched her hair.

– Happy now?

– Do you have to ask?

They kissed, but after a little she drew away.

– What's wrong?

She made herself laugh. – Just worry.

– No one will find us up here, Lucy. We're quite alone.

Later when it grew dark after supper,

– You shouldn't stand against the window like that. You never know who might be looking.

She turned back to face him, laughing.

– The night's so different from London. It never really gets dark there, it's always orange. Here it's so still. The darkness is like velvet, it wraps right round you.

– Round us.

They were making love on the bed. His mouth was close to her ear, whispering something she couldn't hear, didn't care about. She held him tighter, straining him against her. They

17

were lying there, quite still when she registered an unfamiliar noise.

It was a click. He heard it too. There came a light tapping, a squeaking sound, then footsteps.

– Someone in a car?

Lucy had already pulled her clothes on and was sitting, erect, white-faced, on the edge of the bed.

– Maybe one of the forest rangers, come to see what we're doing up here.

– You don't think it might be the police? Don't put on the light.

She restrained his hand but he shook her off.

– They'll have seen the car, Lucy.

– Perhaps they'll go away.

– Perhaps.

They both listened intently to the silence.

– It can't be the police, she exploded. – How could they have found out this soon?

He got off the bed and started to pull on his clothes.

– Don't do anything, Nick. Don't answer them.

The tapping began again. It sounded like someone was walking round the outside of the caravan with a stick. He smiled at her.

– You're not frightened?

They were both bluffing. The tapping stopped. There was a maddeningly long pause, then a creak.

– I'm going to see who it is.

– Nick don't!

He opened the door. There was an explosion and he fell right back across her lap, still warm, shaking. She held him, wondering stupidly for a moment how he could move when he had no face. It was a red mess, compounded flesh and bone where his neck had been.

The silence seemed to last a long time. She didn't feel any need to scream, just all quiet inside. She couldn't stop looking at him, couldn't seem to believe it. She had to though, after a moment she knew it wasn't any dream.

Flanagan was standing in front of her with a shotgun. It

wasn't pointed at her. He was staring at her, leaning on the gun with a kind of easy confidence.

– Nice to see you again, Mrs Scott.

He made a signal with his hand and two other men trooped into the caravan. The thick-set man, whose eyes kept flickering around, was distinctly uncomfortable. And a boy of about twenty, scared stiff, who kept bringing his hand up to his mouth as he stared at her and Nick. She registered all this as if from a very great distance. She had her hands on his shirt, stickily stained with blood, and her fingers kept kneading at his chest, as if, surprised to find it still so warm, she thought she could restore at least a semblance of breathing.

– Where's the money?

Lucy started to laugh. A woman completed the procession, blocking any escape through the door. Flanagan pushed the corpse aside and grabbed Lucy's hair, slapping her across the face while holding her against the wall until she would have slid down in a heap, if there had been room.

– The money's here, Jack, said the thick-set man, lifting the bag from the side.

– Come on, Jack.

The woman's eyes flickered away from Lucy back to the door.

– Did you have to kill him? said the boy in a stupid frightened voice before the thick-set man could shut him up.

– You soft little middle-class bastard, said Flanagan quietly, even amiably.

He pulled Lucy to her feet, then put his arms around her.

– Lovely jewellery Mrs Scott's got. But she should have remembered her wedding ring.

He brought her left arm up beside her face, waved it limply about.

– Now don't struggle.

She screamed as he twisted her arm back.

– I'll show you, Gerald.

– Christ, said the woman at the door, but she didn't move.

The older man retrieved the gun, laid it on the side. He held the boy's arm, warningly. The woman by the door turned away, but kept glancing back. Lucy felt her spine was being broken. Flanagan rammed his fist into her mouth, further than was needed to stop her screaming, so she was choking, gagging, sneezing and blacking out. She was intermittently conscious during the rape, aware when Flanagan got up and there was a sickly blur of light shining through her lids.

She was lying still, tasting but unable to stop the saliva mixed with blood pouring out of her mouth. Flanagan turned round and stared at the thick-set man.

– You next.

George looked slightly askance. His eyes flickered over the girl, then back to Flanagan. Face to face he couldn't demur.

– Might as well, he muttered, and walked slowly across to the bed. Flanagan picked up the gun from the side, and held it seemingly casually. Emma's eyes flickered over the scene. Flanagan poked Gerald in the ribs.

– Now you'll have a chance to prove yourself.

George got up off the bed, avoiding Emma's eyes. He picked up the bag of money, cradling it, until Flanagan took it from him.

– Go on, Gerald.

The boy approached the bed, stared down at the swollen unseeing face and the body lying so limp it appeared almost boneless. He climbed on top of her, lowering himself between her parted thighs. Nothing happened. He lay there for a moment, queasy with horror at the touch of what felt like a corpse. Behind him he could hear Flanagan beginning to chuckle.

– The little sod's a bloody queer. Come on. Stop messing around.

Lucy suddenly came alive and pushed Gerald away. She tried to prop herself up as if about to speak then slumped to one side.

– Get out you lot, said Flanagan. He slung the bag across one shoulder, picked up the gun. – To the car. Move.

He stayed a moment behind them, and struck a match. She watched him stupidly, then was aware that he had gone and had turned the lock. She heard voices from outside, a protesting shout, then the sudden whoosh of flames and the searing consciousness of heat that she knew in a moment would overcome her. She went through the window some-how, rolling clear of the flames already charring and buckling the bodywork. She knew her hands were burned, but her sense of time was confused. She walked away from the fire. When the gas cylinder blew up, she turned back, stunned, to see a blue tower of flame outlining, already consuming, the neighbouring trees. Dim images of the inferno, the funeral pyre, interfered with her progress so she put her blistered hands up in front of her face and howled.

They would never find him in the fire. He was burnt clean away by now, unrecognisable ashes. There was a pain inside her head.

– The devils, she kept muttering, – the devils.

George Ross

George Ross frowned at himself in the mirror as he did up his tie. The collar wouldn't lie down straight. He shrugged, and pulled at the lapels of his jacket till it sat better on his shoulders. His hair was greying; his face heavily-lined and unemotional. He turned round. His flat, at the edge of a sixties' overspill estate, looked out onto open country.

He closed the window and carefully locked it tight, picked up his shopping list from the table, and stood for a moment looking at the pile of envelopes on the far edge. There were seven; all typewritten with his name and address. He'd re-ceived one every day for the last seven days. Each had con-tained a plain white card, nothing more. Today the card had been black.

He gathered them up, tore them across and threw them in the bin. He would be late if he didn't go now. The shopping list went in one pocket. He double-locked the door behind him, hurried down the stairs. It was ten past six.

He drew into the supermarket car park at half-past. He was meeting his wife's solicitor at seven, but the office was only a few minutes' drive away. He thought of getting a cup of coffee, but was too edgy to settle. He leaned on the wall outside the chemist's and lit a cigarette. He wasn't easily rattled, but those cards upset him.

They had made him feel vulnerable. He exhaled. It was just a crazy practical joke; he had nothing to worry about. Whoever sent them had probably picked his name at random from a list. Just someone with stamps to waste. He had thought of asking his neighbours if they had received anything similar, but had shrunk from doing so. He could not help wondering about the person who had sent the cards. Did they get a thrill each morning when they knew the post would be delivered? Did they work themselves up trying to gauge his reaction day by day, at first baffled and contemptuous, then gradually growing into fear? He had scanned the open fields beyond his window for any sign that someone was watching him. But taking those kind of measures and being careful to lock his windows and doors, gave him an uneasy feeling that he was colluding with his persecutor, effectively frightening himself better than anyone else could hope to do.

He was a powerful man. But against certain kinds of threat physical strength didn't count for very much.

His mind went back two years. There had never been any repercussions from that business in the forest. It had taken them all night to put out the fire; a couple of acres of trees were completely destroyed. He had driven up there last spring. Two years' rainfall had settled the ash and the undergrowth was coming through freshly green beneath the rows of saplings. He'd parked his car and looked around. The police had been satisfied that a faulty gas cylinder had started the fire. Cold sweat pricked George's skin as he remembered how he had gone to the police to give them a description of the caravan he sold and the couple who bought it. Only the thought of Flanagan in the car outside waiting to drive him home had made him able to go through with it.

Although nothing more had come of it, he'd had an uneasy moment or two since then. Remembering the rape, he told himself he'd been caught up in events beyond his control, but he still felt bad. He'd only gone into it for the money, but that he'd never seen. Flanagan had stayed around just long enough, telling him to wait, then had disappeared. George tossed away the stub, and started to walk towards the supermarket. He always did his shopping on Tuesdays, part of a tacit agreement with his ex-wife that they would avoid each other.

Also it was less busy. He collected a trolley and drew the list out of his pocket. He went round the shelves methodically, collecting mostly tins, a packet of rice, tea. He picked up a large bottle of whisky and two pork pies. He couldn't see the point of buying anything else. As he pushed his trolley slowly towards the checkout, it was ten to seven.

The girl behind the till he always went to smiled at him.

– You're late tonight.

– Traffic was bad.

She wrapped the whisky in a heavy brown paper bag and handed it to him.

– Makes me glad I don't drive.

– Well, he said. – You can't have much luck with the buses round here.

– I don't go anywhere very often.

There was a brief pause as she met his eyes. For a moment George Ross was tongue-tied. She was a pretty blonde with a good figure. A sense of his loneliness welled up inside him.

– Thirteen pounds thirteen.

He gave her two ten pound notes. Another girl came up, saying

– Time to go home, Lucy.

The blonde girl laughed.

– I'll just give him his change.

She caught George's eye and he joined in. Her cool hands touched his as she counted out the coins, then gave him a fiver. She got up from the stool as he was packing his groceries away, and he heard the whirring of the till as she turned the key to roll through the receipts. He paused a moment, then said

– See you next week.

– I hope so, Mr Ross.

Pushing his trolley away he heard their laughter and wished that he'd kept quiet.

Six minutes to seven. He reached his car and loaded the shopping into the boot. He slammed it shut. The first time it bounced open and he swore, which made him realise how jittery he was. He didn't want to go to this meeting. He pulled his tie loose round his neck and passed his hands over his hair. He hated his wife's solicitor. He couldn't afford to pay any more alimony. They seemed to calculate the payments on the basis of their own fat fees, not what he earned.

As he drove out of the car park, a blonde figure emerged just to his left and began to walk briskly along the pavement. He braked a little too suddenly. She turned as if instinctively to see what had made the noise. He raised a hand from the wheel. She smiled. He leaned across and wound down the window.

– Can I give you a lift?

– That's very nice of you.

She slid in. She was carrying a large bag, almost a suitcase, which she kept on her lap.

– Where do you live?

– Some way out of town.

He felt emboldened by the casualness of her tone.

– Isn't it rather inconvenient for you to get to work?

She measured him with her glance. – I manage.

They were quiet until the car stopped at some traffic lights.

– Look, he said – I know... you wouldn't like to go for a drink?

His hands were sweating.

– I don't like pubs.

He couldn't keep himself from wondering what she might do if he tried to kiss her.

– Your name's Lucy, isn't it?

– You heard the other girl at the check out say it.

– Yes, he nodded. – It's always been one of my favourite names.

– That's sweet of you.

She opened her bag to take out a pack of cigarettes. He

24

noticed her hands shake as she tried to strike a match and indicated the lighter on the dashboard.

– Occupational hazard.

She sat back on the seat and drew a deep breath. They'd reached the bypass at the edge of the town.

– You haven't told me which way you want to go.

He thought her eyes were blue as she turned to look at him.

– I'd like to go to the sea, she said softly.

– I'll take you.

She smiled to check the eagerness in his tone. – I was only dreaming, she said lightly. – You'd better drop me off here. I can get a bus from round the corner.

He reached for her wrist, gripped it.

– I wouldn't have thought you were that type.

He released it.

– Why to look at you, she went on – you'd think you were a nice, married, middle-aged man.

She put her hand in her bag quite casually and brought out a gun. He felt it jab into his ribs.

– Now you can drive me to the seaside, Mr Ross. And if you make any move at all be assured that I will kill you without the least regard for my own safety.

He felt himself beginning to laugh, at first dryly, then hysterically as the metal dug deeper into his side.

– This is a joke, some kind of joke. Why you must know that I didn't mean you any harm.

– That's right.

He heard the gun cock and started the car.

– I just wanted to ask you a few questions, Mr Ross. Where's Flanagan?

– He disappeared. He went to London perhaps, how should I know?

– Keep driving, Mr Ross.

– Why are you doing this?

She laughed.– When we get there, I'll tell you all about it.

In the fading evening sun two figures and a car were silhouetted against the sky on the clifftop. Lucy raised the gun against Ross's head. The trigger gave a soft click that was succeeded by a moment of silence.

– It wasn't loaded!

He screamed at her.

– It never was. You drove all the way out here at the point of a toy gun, Mr Ross. But I had some strange desire to prove to myself that you could be frightened: now it's a double blow when you see that you were scared of nothing at all.

She tossed the nickel gun at his feet. – Don't you want to do something, Mr Ross? As you see I'm a defenceless female at your mercy. Won't you finish what your friends tried to do in the caravan? You've already destroyed my life, why not kill me, too?

She turned and began to walk away along the cliff path. As he watched her his heart beat so fast he thought he was about to collapse. He slumped inside the car, unsure what to do next. The keys were still in the ignition. He turned them, and the car shot backwards over the edge of the cliff.

Lucy turned round. She ran quickly back along the path and looked down. The car lay smashed on the rocks below with the high tide lapping around. It would be carried out to sea in due course. She had timed it well. Two weeks later, when the car and body had been found and reported in the local press, the police received an envelope. Inside was a white postcard with three lines plainly typed.

GEORGE ROSS

RAPIST MURDERER

THE FIRST ONE

Mandy

Mandy stared at the dirty bricks in the wall across the street. She let her eye run along automatically, arranging them into patterns, or tracing the stain from a pipe or a particular smudge that ran down like a ripple of smoke. She looked right through the pedestrians, preferring the ones who ignored her to those who glanced slyly aside or nudged each other as if daring themselves to make an approach. She was standing in the doorway of a cinema. From time to time men pushed past her, coming out or going in. She ignored them too, except when an angry voice yelled at her to come inside and sell tickets. She was tall and dark and wore a black top and pink mini-skirt. She had two fake tattoos of butterflies on her arms. They served to highlight the muscles underneath; Mandy went to judo classes which had stood her in good stead a few times.

A woman was walking along slowly, looking around her as if lost. She wore a green belted coat, and a beret squashed rather too far down on her head. Mandy froze as the woman looked straight at her. It was an empty, shocked face before she recognised her. Then she smiled.

– Mandy, is that you?

– Yes, it's me, Lucy, Mandy said after a little while.

The woman had set down her suitcase helplessly in the middle of the street.

– I can't believe this.

Suddenly she swayed as if about to fall. When Mandy ran forward to hold her up, Lucy clung to her. Mandy could feel her heat beating very fast. She picked up the suitcase with her free hand and with her other arm round Lucy led her into the cinema and made her sit on the chair in the box office while she made some tea.

Life seemed to come back into Lucy's eyes as she drank it.

– Do you work here? she said, looking round at the posters that lined the walls.

– Yes, said Mandy. – Quite a change from the restaurant.

– Is it? Lucy replied softly, but there was an edge of bitterness either in her smile or in her voice.

Mandy leaned against the door. There was barely room for the two of them in that space.

– Why have you come back here? Someone else may recognise you.

– Tony's still around then?

Lucy smiled faintly.

– When he found out what you'd done he wanted your head.

– I can't blame him, said Lucy. She stared at Mandy

27

intently. – Will you help me?

Mandy felt a faint prickle of unease. – Help you? With what? she repeated.

Lucy smiled gently. – Perhaps it's better if you don't ask.

– To do with Tony? Mandy persisted nevertheless.

Lucy looked slightly pained. – I suppose you could say it was to do with the money.

Then her voice changed. – Do you know a man called Flanagan?

Mandy hesitated fractionally. – Why?

Lucy shrugged. – I just want to meet him, that's all. Someone told me he might be in London.

Putting down the cup, she rose to her feet. – I'd better go now. Thanks for the tea.

– Wait, Lucy.

Mandy didn't move from in front of the door. – I can't let you go like this. You're not well. Here's the key to my flat, it's close by. At least you can get some rest. I'll be back about eleven. We can talk then if you like, see what we can do.

Mandy stood just inside the door of the darkened bedroom, listening for the soft, regular breathing from the couch on the other side that would tell her Lucy was asleep. She heard a sigh, then a creak as if Lucy had turned over, a low noise that sounded like muttered words, then another, more peaceful sigh. She tiptoed back to bed and shook Phil awake, with her hand over his mouth.

– What the fuck's the matter now?

– Don't put on the light. She'll see. I've got to talk to you.

– Well give me a cigarette, Mandy.

She passed him the packet and a box of matches, sat down on the bed while he lit it and took the first few drags.

– That's nice, that white dressing gown.

She felt his hand slip inside it and got up irritably.

– You smoke this place out.

She went across to open the window. Neon signs in the street outside flickered on and off, irregularly.

– I have to smoke when I'm thinking.

She turned round. – Well you'd better start thinking

28

quickly. Lucy wants to rent a room.

– Here?

– No, thickhead. Like that room that last girl left in such a hurry, I can't think why.

Phil stubbed out his cigarette and lit another. – I can't see what's so unusual about that.

– She want to rent it by the day. She'll pay fifty pounds.

He was silent for a moment, then said – Well that's fair enough.

– You know it's better than fair. That's the problem.

– Tell her it's okay. I'll show her round tomorrow.

– Phil!

– Shut up. I want to get some sleep.

He rolled himself up in the sheet, turned to face away from her. She stood by the window for a moment, then cast off the white dressing gown and slipped in beside him. For a minute she listened to his irritated breathing, then he rolled back and stared at her.

– Fifty pounds a day, he said – for us. The last girl paid her rent till the end of the month. And paying that much, she's not going to want it for long, is she?

His eyes gleamed.

– Smart boy, said Mandy softly. Then – I thought you wanted to sleep.

– I changed my mind.

– This is the room.

Phil had led Lucy up two flights of stairs. When he opened the door, she seemed to hesitate, then entered boldly enough.

– Can you get rid of this furniture?

She gently kicked a cane seat with rose-patterned cushions. The dressing table had gauzes draped around. She undid the ribbons that held them back, drew them out at arm's length experimentally.

– What's this supposed to be?

She lifted down a picture.

– People like them. You've got to have some furniture.

– Well leave it all then. I don't care.

29

She walked across the room and looked out of the window.
– Is there a maid?
– Rose. You'll meet her soon enough.
She nodded. – I'll stay here.
– Is there anything else you want?
She sat down on the bed. – Just leave me alone, Phil.
– She's not exactly friendly, said Phil to Mandy, who turned round from where she was fixing her hair.
– I don't see what you're complaining about.
He came up behind her and ran his hands down the sides of her tight dress.
– You'll spoil it.
– What's she planning to do with that room?
– She didn't tell me.
– You're sure about that?
She freed herself from his grasp. – She's not well, she said abruptly.
– Then why doesn't she buy herself a rest cure in a hospital?
– Can't you mind your own business for five minutes, she burst out.
He moved up behind her and put his hands round so one rested on her ribs and the other on her crotch. She stared at their reflection in the mirror, his hands white, flecked with dark hair, against the green.

Lucy kept to herself. The door to her room was usually locked and there was no reply.
– You'll have to speak to her about that.
– Speak to her yourself.
– What is it between you?
Mandy shrugged. – She's my friend, that's all.
– She used to be your boss, Phil went on. – Was she like this then?
– No, Mandy allowed. Then she was silent.
– Has she asked you about Flanagan again?
– No!
This time it was almost a groan. She rolled over and buried her face in the pillow. Phil put his hand on her shoulder and

shook her.

– For ten days no one has been inside that room. Rose goes up there every morning to clean, but Lucy won't let her in. Rose says that no one else has been up there. If she doesn't work how the fuck does she get the kind of money she's paying me?

– She stole it, said Mandy simply – from the restaurant, she added, watching the effect.

– That was her? Phil's voice changed. – How much?

Mandy regretted having told him. She shrugged, with an instinct to play it down. – I don't know. Couple of thousand, perhaps.

Phil said – Don't hold out on me.

– I really don't know, she repeated. She watched him. – So you don't have to worry about her doing anything illegal now.

Phil got out of bed, started to pull on his clothes.

– Where are you going?

He turned round, still buttoning up his shirt, and smiled.

– That was quite a business, three years back. I can remember Tony going on about the bitch who stole his money. He used to say about all the things he'd like to do with her if ever he found her...

– Phil, no.

– Don't worry, I won't tell him. But he offered a reward, didn't he. It must still stand. I can just go to the police.

He smiled. – The due processes of the law can take their course.

She was silent, thinking. – We're involved.

– Not any more.

A shadow crossed her face as he looked at her.

– Wait, she said uncertainly as he turned to go. – Let me go up there and talk to her. Perhaps we can sort something out without having to go to the police.

She stared at Phil. – You come too.

A clock was striking noon as they crossed the street and walked the few steps. The card 'Model' immediately caught Mandy's eye. As they climbed the uncarpeted stairs, Phil got hold of Mandy's wrist and squeezed it roughly. She shook free.

– If she won't answer we go straight to the police.

They reached the second floor. Phil hesitated outside the door, then put his eye to the keyhole.

– There's something blocking the other side.

– Probably the key.

He looked round at her impatiently, then raised his hand and knocked. There was no reply. He waited, then battered again, so the door shook in its frame.

– Call her.

– Lucy! Lucy! Mandy whispered, then in a louder voice.

The door on the landing below opened and Rose's head peeped out. She put a finger to her lips and crept upstairs.

– There's someone in there. She's gone out.

– She what! Phil exploded.

– Just a minute ago, to get some fags. She asked me to make sure that he didn't leave.

Mandy glanced from Phil to Rose.

– How long's he been in there?

– She brought him in herself. About an hour ago.

Rose spoke in a stage whisper. – She had music on really loud. I was watching TV, and had to turn the volume right up to hear. Then five minutes ago, all went quiet and she came down.

– So she should be back any minute.

Rose nodded. They all stood there on the landing; Phil edgy, Mandy worried, Rose apprehensive but enjoying the excitement. Then

– Ten minutes, said Mandy suddenly. – She isn't coming back.

– Is there someone in there? said Phil to Rose.

She shrugged. – I saw him come in.

– You wouldn't have heard him leave if you had the telly on, Mandy burst out impatiently. She turned to Phil. – You can go and get the police now if you like. There's something wrong in there, really wrong, I know.

Phil spoke slowly. – If there is I don't really want to get mixed up with it. Neither do you …

– I think we're already in it up to our necks.

She turned abruptly to Rose. – You've got a key. Well, fetch it. Do something you're paid for for a change.

She picked up a thin piece of rod from the floor and squinted down the hollow tube.

– She could have used this to turn the key from the outside. And whoever's in there won't, or can't …

She thrust the rod into the lock. There was the sound of the key falling to the carpet on the other side.

They waited for the sound of an outraged voice. Phil put his hand up to his cheek. They stared at each other, there on the landing. Then Mandy wrinkled her nose.

– What's that smell? said Phil hoarsely.

Rose came back with the key. Mandy faltered, then they all pushed at once into the room.

A man was sitting in one of the cane chairs, naked from the waist down except for the bonds that lashed his ankles firmly to its legs. His wrists were bound to its arms. The rose-patterned cushions were scorched, with long dark splashes where some liquid had not yet dried. An empty bottle of perfume stood on the table beside him.

– Who is it? Phil whispered when he found his voice.

Mandy gagged and brought her hand up to her mouth.

– How can I tell when he has no face?

The sound of her voice seemed to revive the man. One of the hands attempted to move. With horror the spectators registered that the remains of the blistered lips were twitching, speaking. Then the head flopped forward.

– Get an ambulance, Rose. Move!

– He's dead, said Phil tonelessly when she had gone.

Mandy stepped forward. – She didn't do this. Who could do this?

Phil met her eyes warily. Something seemed to attract his attention; he pointed to a white square of card pinned to the man's chest. Mandy retrieved it, shuddering as the pin came out, and turned it over.

– Let me see.

But she jerked away from him and concealing the card in

33

her hand she let out a low wail. – I didn't believe her. I didn't think she would.

She put her hands up to her face.

– Flanagan! said Phil, stooping to retrieve the card from where it fell. He stared up at her. – You knew. You knew all the time.

– Not till now.

When she took her hands away from her face it was like a white shadow.

– How long do you think Rose will be?

Then they heard the thin wail of the ambulance rise above the other noises in the street.

– Got a match?

She struck it shakily. Phil watched in silence as she burned the card and rubbed the thin crisp into ash between her fingers.

Gerald Pascoe R.I.P.

The entrance hall of the clinic was filled with flowering plants. Their damp scent hung in the air, mixing oddly with the disinfectant.

Adele sat behind the reception desk, trying to check the accounts. Her head ached from lack of sleep and every so often she would move over to the sink and splash her face with cold water. It was as she was drying her dripping face with a towel that she heard a slight cough and glancing in the mirror saw a woman standing behind her on the far side of the counter.

– The door was open, she said apologetically.

Adele smiled, rather self-consciously putting down the towel.

– It's too hot in here with it closed.

– It's just like a greenhouse. Do you look after all these plants?

– When I haven't got anything else to do.

She wanted to get on with her work. She smiled at the stranger, hoping to get her to tell what she wanted, but the woman had fallen silent and was glancing nervously around as if completely at a loss.

– Can I help you, said Adele at last, as gently as she could.

The woman looked up. For a second Adele registered a hopeless bewilderment in her eyes.

– This is an AIDS clinic?

Adele barely nodded.

– I'm looking for someone called Gerald Pascoe, she brought the words out with difficulty – I was told he was here.

Adele looked at her. – I think you ought to sit down.

She came out from behind the counter and guided her across the room to the armchairs. Only when they were seated did she say

– Gerald Pascoe died this morning.

She'd had to do it a hundred times but sticking to the routine didn't make it any better. She waited for the reaction, not looking at Lucy's face but noticing that the hands on the arms of the chair suddenly gripped so tight that the knuckles stood out pale.

– He was so young, she whispered.

– He was a drug addict, Adele said simply, looking down at her own hands.

Then she got up. – Can I get you anything, she said awkwardly, wanting to brush the moment aside. – Miss...

– Lucy Snow, said the other woman abruptly.

– Miss Snow, said Adele, somehow confused and aware she was doing it all wrong – I'm sorry, terribly sorry, at a time like this, but I'm afraid I have to ask you some questions.

– What questions?

Her face was pale, anguished. She stood up, stretching her hands out towards Adele in an unconscious gesture of denial.

– I'm sorry he's dead, she whispered. – Believe me.

– Miss Snow, said Adele awkwardly – I ...

She laid her hand on Lucy's arm. For a moment she felt the incredible tension and then the woman seemed to relax.

– I'm sorry, she said, and managed a little smile. – I was just a friend of Gerald's, that's all.

It was a day of bright sunshine at the little village church. Mrs Pascoe, dressed in black, was supported by her husband as they walked behind their son's coffin. His sister was silent and sullen behind them. As she walked, listening irritably to the sound of her mother's sobs, she glanced furtively round from underneath the veil they'd made her wear and spotted a stranger standing by the gate, who appeared to be watching them. A blonde woman, dressed in shorts and a halter top and eating an ice cream, she looked like a hippy tourist.

Jean Pascoe sighed. She'd wanted to go down to the beach, but her father had threatened to cut off her allowance if she didn't come. She stared drearily at the earth falling on her brother's coffin. When it was over they had turned to walk back down the path when suddenly Jean said

– The flowers. Who sent that enormous wreath of white lilies?

Her father glared at her.

– No Mum, Jean said impatiently. – I mean we know who sent the other flowers. They were all family. But those lilies... I mean Gerald didn't exactly have any friends who'd do something like that.

Mrs Pascoe's sobs increased. Her father stared at Jean.

– If you're so curious, he said slowly in a voice that shook with anger – you can go back and read the card.

Jean ran lightly back up the path. They were still filling in the grave, and the wreath of lilies glowed jewel-like against the dark earth. As she bent down she smelt the heavy crushed lingering hothouse scent. The petals felt like wax to touch. She found the envelope, hidden among the twisted leaves, and ripped it open.

Her shouts echoed through the churchyard to where her parents were getting into their car.

– Mum! Dad!

She flew down the path, her veil tugging in the wind. As her father turned to explode at her she thrust the pasteboard into his hand.

– Daddy, Daddy!

She seemed genuinely frightened. – What does it mean?

Mr Pascoe turned the slip over slowly. It read
'GERALD PASCOE
MURDERER RAPIST'
And that was all.

Harry

The shore was black with seaweed, deserted except for a few people with their dogs. It was towards the end of September, and the tourists had long gone. At low tide, the bulk of the pier dominated the beach, more solid than the land around it which shifted gradually with every year. Its massive spans were bolted together to withstand the tides, the winter winds, and the salt mists. Gulls had colonised them. Some rose squawking at the approach of excited dogs, but they soon settled again.

The young man leaning on the rail of the esplanade watched a young woman as she emerged from between the iron spans and walked briskly along the sand. She caught his interest for a moment and his gaze followed her automatically. He couldn't make out much except that she had fair hair and wore a red coat which made a brilliant splash of colour against the bleached, muddy greys and browns. She carried a file of papers under her arm and kept stopping to readjust them as they were whipped by the wind out of place and threatened to blow away. He turned his head a little; she'd altered direction and was heading for the esplanade. He saw her climb up the next flight of steps along and stand on the kerb, waiting for the lights to change so she could get across. She kept pushing her hair back as the wind disarranged it. He watched her cross the road and vanish up a lane between two palatial, crumbling hotels. It would bring her out on the main shopping street, but what would she do then? He pushed her from his mind and started to walk back in the direction of the pier, then abruptly crossed the road and headed up past scrubby salt-blasted trees, into the centre of town.

The bar was still open in the afternoons. A few weeks ago it had been crowded, even in the quiet time, but now it was deserted. Glancing around, Jim thought that after this week they wouldn't bother to open at all. He gazed at the photographs and prints that lined the walls. They were all of wrestlers. A slightly ironic smile touched his face, he shook his head, and taking a soft cloth he started to dust the ones nearest him, carefully adjusting those which had been knocked out of line by a careless elbow. Then he heard the door open, and swung round. A woman stood there, looking at him.

– You are open?

– Yes.

He put the duster down and went back behind the bar. She walked over, slowly, diffidently glancing about her and sat down on a stool.

– Crème de menthe, please.

She was hesitantly polite. – And won't you have something yourself?

As he poured himself an orange juice, he noticed her looking at him.

– You could have had something more than that.

He put the glass down. – I don't drink, love, he said. – Can't stand the taste of it, working all day in here.

She smiled at him. – Yes, she said – I can understand that. I've been admiring your pictures, she went on after a little pause and several sips from the glass. – You see, I really should be straight with you. I didn't come in here just by chance, but because I heard that this would be the place to find out some things I wanted to know.

Jim's face was impassive but his voice when he spoke was guarded.

– What kind of things?

He went back to polishing the pictures.

– I'm a journalist. I was hoping to put together a really strong feature piece.

– What about?

– Women wrestlers.

He froze slightly and frowned as she caught his eye.

– There's one in particular I'm looking for. Emma Honey.
He laughed.
– I know she comes from round here.
– She's still here all right.
He put down the cloth. – She'll never talk to you.
Lucy produced a file full of photocopies. – Can you take a look at these?
He wiped his hands, accepted it.
– Yes, these are all her. They're going back a bit. 19...71?
He checked the date at the top of a clipping. – She must have retired about then.
– What does she do now?
– I don't know as she does anything much. She dropped out of sight for a while, then reappeared a couple of years ago. Her son wrestles now.
He pulled a face.
– No good? said Lucy quickly.
– Emma breaks her heart every time he loses.
He put the file down awkwardly on the counter. Lucy avoided his eyes. She tucked the papers under her arm again, gave him a quick smile, and finished her drink. Jim felt uneasily that he'd given away more than he knew. When she'd gone out, he stood still for a moment, puzzled and almost jumped when the door swung back again.
– What's the matter, Jim? said the young man from the esplanade. – You look like you've seen a ghost.
Jim cleared his throat. – Harry, he said – there's been a woman in here asking questions about your mother.

The night club was decorated with panels of sixties' stars, banded with mirrors that flashed as the lights swung round above the heads of the dancers. At the far end was a raised area with tables from which you could look down on all this or, drawing further back where they were screened by a trellis of fake greenery, be private.
Harry was kissing Jane as they danced too slowly, out of step with the others, near the edge of the floor. Her lips under his were warm and soothing. She linked her arms behind his

back and leaned against him.

– I'll die if I dance any more.

– Better go home, then.

She laughed, pressed close against him. – I'm so thirsty, darling, she whispered. – Just one drink and then we'll go.

– I'll get you some juice.

– With vodka in it, she murmured, running her hands down his back. She sat down at one of the tables while he went to the bar. He glanced back but didn't catch her eye. She was wearing a red strapless dress that looked beautiful against her skin.

But when he came back with the drinks she wasn't there. He stared round, thinking at first that he'd mistaken the table. The woman at the next one looked up at him and smiled.

– You Harry?

He put the glasses on the empty table. – Where's Jane?

– She asked me to give you a message, that she had to go, and she's very sorry. Next Monday, if that means anything to you, which I suppose it does.

She kept looking down at her nails, smiling slightly. She wore a dark blue dress with a line of silver round the neck and no sleeves. He stared at her blonde hair and the tiny glass of emerald liquid in front of her.

– Are you with someone?

– No.

She shook her head.

– Do you mind if I join you?

She smiled, looking down again.

– Let's go to a table at the back, she said. – It's quieter. We can't hear ourselves think.

He picked up the glasses and followed her across. – It seems an odd place to come to think, he said when they were seated between the trellises.

– I like watching people, she said simply.

He laughed. – I shouldn't think you'd find anyone here very interesting.

Lucy looked down. – It's the little things that are interesting. The details that go to make up the pattern of their life.

She spread her hands wide. – If you were studying someone, that's what you'd look for. Once you have that pattern,
you can be fairly sure they won't step outside it.

He laughed. – Sounds like you're a policewoman.

She fiddled with her glass. – I work in a dress shop in the
centre of town.

– Jennifer's?

She nodded.

– That must be why I think I've seen you somewhere before.

She looked up for a moment but he was smiling.

– I must be boring you.

– Not at all, he said. – I was just wondering what conclu-
sions you've come to about me.

She raised her glass. – I've only known you five minutes.

– Evasion.

She put the glass down and stared at him.

– You laugh too much. So you're unhappy.

– Not a very risky guess.

She shrugged. – I don't know what you want.

He looked at her.

– You're a strange person, she said abruptly. – I can't make
you out at all.

– Does it bother you?

– No, she said quickly.

He was still looking at her. – I'm supposed to be a wrestler,
he said in an even, matter-of-fact tone. – But I can't wrestle.
I'm terrible.

– Why do you do it then?

– Because of my mother.

She kept staring at the table.

– Is there nothing else you'd like to do?

– Do you know I really haven't given it much thought.

– Can't you quit anyway?

This time she raised her eyes and saw him looking at her
ironically.

– When I have a good excuse. When I'm too badly injured
to wrestle again.

– But you might be in pain for the rest of your life.

– There are worse things than pain.

She stared up at him as if he'd said something that had profoundly shocked her. He had the smile ready on his lips but it faded when he saw how serious she looked.

– I do believe you mean it, she said softly.

– Perhaps you think that's strange as well.

– No.

She shook her head vigorously.

– Well, you could be right, he said casually, conscious he didn't want to pursue it any further.

She smiled, playing with her glass so it caught the light and flashed green reflections over the table, herself, and him.

– Perhaps you'll tell me now why you've been asking questions about my mother.

The glass toppled over, spreading a sticky puddle across the cloth, and Lucy's face flushed from being very pale so he could see the blood burn in her cheeks. He mopped at the liquid to stop it running onto her dress, as she sat there quite still, making no move to help herself.

– Why... she said eventually.

– Just tell me what you want with my mother. Jimmy didn't think you were a journalist, and neither do I.

She stared at him. – I can't tell you.

He started to rise. – Well goodbye then.

– No, please wait!

Her hand shot out and lightly touched his arm. – Please, she said. – I don't want you to go, really I don't.

The expression on her face was scared, almost pleading. He sat down.

– I'll tell you, she said. – But you may find you don't want to know.

Emma Honey

Emma Honey owned a house some way out in the suburbs that sprawled along the coast. The week she'd spent there alone since she'd last seen her son had made her feel that she was approaching a crisis in her life.

42

She had two things on her mind as she wandered round her house; they kept crossing and overlapping so that buffeted by the two, she was in danger of going crazy. She wandered from room to room, opening and shutting the doors, touching the furniture to reassure herself that her surroundings were real. In some indefinable way the house haunted her. She thought of all the years when a place of her own had been the dream that had kept her going. She had believed financial security would take some of the worry out of her life, providing the base for a future where the horrors of what she called to herself 'the bad time' could be forgotten at last. But security crumbled before the blow she'd been dealt in the past week. Her son, who she'd loved and trusted; the only person, she told herself, who had ever meant anything to her, had disappeared, and sick with worry as she was after a few days, it seemed even worse when she finally received his card with a view of the Carpet Gardens, Eastbourne, and the brief, enigmatic message that he had decided to get married and was bringing his wife home. It didn't strike her as exactly out of character; he had a stubborn streak which could make him go all out for what he wanted without paying much heed to the consequences. Emma shifted uneasily as she thought how in the past she'd taken advantage of the fact that he was so unwilling to hurt her. The thought that he might have changed struck her as stupid, but somehow she found she couldn't help but regard this marriage as a strange challenge to herself. I'll change, she swore softly to herself, immediately aware of her hypocrisy. Things aren't going to be the same; to try to pretend would be the quickest way to drive him away. Neither of us is stupid, let's be civilised about the whole thing. She found herself able to laugh. It was a relief, but the sound of her laugh shocked her and she made an effort to pull herself together. She stared into a mirror, noticing her wild hair, the clothes dirty and untucked, her face tired, sagging.

– This is no good, she muttered to herself. Then she thought
– Let the pretty girl see me like this.

The image of her son's bride, made up of smooth hair and skin, perfume and floating bright clothes, depressed her. She turned away from the mirror, washed her face, and put on fresh clothes.

The doorbell rang uncertainly as if someone had pressed their finger to the buzzer then jerked it away. In a moment Emma was on the stairs, then she hesitated as looking down through the hall she saw the double shadow beyond the frosted panel of the door and heard the neat chink of keys as they were finally fitted into the lock. The door opened. Harry came in first, carrying the suitcase. He looked up at Emma, smiled quickly and turned back. The other half of the shadow stepped inside, hiding herself with the door until she was in the hall when Harry gently pushed it shut behind her.

Emma found the use of her legs and came down the stairs. In the silence she felt her heart thumping unpleasantly. Harry waited till she'd crossed the hall before he said

– Mum, this Lucy. Lucy, my mother.

Emma held out her hand. Looking at them together, as a couple, she saw her son, dark, rather saturnine, heavily built, and this blonde creature with her pale skin, wearing crimson – unusual for a blonde – thought Emma momentarily, the grey eyes half-shut but opening wider as she felt the pressure of Emma's hand, and Emma herself feeling a little shock of reaction as she sensed something hidden in the girl, a fibre of steel, a toughness that surprised her and made her smile more than she was expecting to, eliciting an almost puzzled glance in response from those half-veiled eyes.

– I'm sorry I missed your wedding.

– I'm sorry I didn't invite you, Harry said, glancing from one to the other. Emma had been aware of his eyes on her, sardonically, throughout. – I didn't think you liked weddings.

– Once in a while I might make an exception, said Emma – for my own son.

She heard the girl's voice for the first time.

– It was a very sudden decision.

– Very sudden, said Harry. It struck Emma, all tuned up, that a strange glance passed between him and Lucy.

– I haven't been to Eastbourne in a long time, she said abruptly.

– You know what these places are like in autumn, Mum. Sad, and empty, and lonely.

She caught the edge of another glance.

– The perfect place for a honeymoon, when you want to be alone.

– I'd have thought that if you waited a bit longer you could have gone somewhere nicer. Italy, France.

– I spent my first honeymoon in Cyprus, said the girl quietly. – That didn't work out, I prefer Eastbourne.

While Emma stared at her she actually took Harry's hand and squeezed it.

– Are you from round here? said Emma, confused.

– From London.

– She works in Jennifer's, Mum, said Harry, who'd at some point released his hand. He glanced at his wife – Don't you?

– Yes, said Lucy simply, not looking at anyone.

– And how did you two meet?

– In a nightclub, said Lucy quickly. Emma saw her son smile as if something had amused him.

– Any more questions? he said as she caught his eye.

Emma shook her head. He took her arm to lead her through to the living-room.

– Cheer up. She's a nice girl. Doesn't smoke, drinks only a little, saves her money. No major vices, have you, dear?

– Only one, said Lucy quietly.

Emma was struck by the edge in Harry's voice. She glanced round.

The girl bit her lip and flushed. She avoided Emma's eyes.

Harry seemed to have no inclination to move out. – We can't afford it, he said, – and why? There's plenty of room here.

Strangely enough, Emma thought, Lucy agreed with him. She gave up her furnished room near the centre of town, though it meant a long journey for her each day to get to work. Emma remembered the unease, almost pity, she'd felt when Lucy finally transported her belongings over to the house. They were contained in two bags. There was something uncanny, Emma thought, about a life which in close on thirty years had amassed no more than that. Awkwardly, she'd offered to help Lucy unpack. The offer had been declined, but somehow things had worked out so that Emma was standing in the room, talking to her son, while Lucy laid out the neatly folded garments on the bed, giving each a little shake before transferring it to the wardrobe or the drawer. Emma was uneasy about curiosity, she felt indulgence in it almost a weakness, but she tried furtively to sneak a glimpse of what Lucy was unfolding. Peering past Lucy's elbows, the shape she made as she moved from wardrobe to bed, she saw nothing that could interest her, no photos, nothing remotely personal nestling in the folds of material, just a toothbrush and a few little bottles and jars. A slight movement made her aware of her son, who'd also fallen silent. She looked towards where he leaned against the door, studying the restless lines of his face and the eyes that never seemed to waver from the slender body of his wife. They had an expression she'd never seen before. Then he seemed aware that he was being watched, stiffening then relaxing almost in one breath.

– Aren't you nearly finished, Lucy? We could go out.

Emma heard Lucy's voice replying as she closed the door behind her.

She went downstairs and made herself a strong cup of coffee, all the while the thought tracking round in her head.

– He's crazy about her.

Her hand shook. – Being like that about anyone.

She shut herself in the living-room, switched on the TV to cut out her thoughts, but it kept coming back.

– Something's badly wrong.

She couldn't get it out of her head. The image of the girl as she'd seen her on the first day, like ice and flame, the white face and pale hair rising up out of the crimson burst of the dress that was like the heart of a fire. And steel inside.

– She has no heart, Emma muttered to herself – no feelings. Or she wouldn't let him be unhappy.

She hated herself all the time that she was walking over to the cupboard and pouring whisky into her coffee. She almost forced herself to struggle against raising the cup to her mouth, inhaling the bitter contrasting smells, then swallowing it gratefully without giving herself time to taste it. She needed something to get rid of the terrible chill she felt inside; the mixture of worry and guilt that when she woke suddenly and uneasily at half past two in the darkest part of the night, threatened to consume her.

Some days she didn't see Lucy at all. Other times, on her way to bed, she'd hear the familiar click of the front door, and would pause, cat-footed as she was in spite of her weight, on the landing to glimpse down into the hall where Lucy would be standing, always in the dark as if she was afraid of waking someone by putting on the light. There was something oddly tired and reflective in her attitude as she was still for a moment before taking off her coat. Emma never addressed her on these occasions, just observed her for a minute, then vanished into her room as she heard Lucy beginning to climb the stairs.

Then one morning she went into the kitchen and sniffed the raw smell of spirits in the air. Harry's back was to her, standing by the sink, as he poured the bottle of whisky away.

– Come on now, he said without turning as if he'd heard her come in.

– This isn't like you.

She stood frozen, with a sense of shame. There was a host of bottles by the sink, all the alcohol he could find in the house.

– You'll kill yourself if you go on like this. You know what the doctor said to you, that carrying your weight you shouldn't drink at all.

He came over to her, shook her gently by the arm.

– I'm listening to you, she said roughly.

– You always said to me, he went on – you used to really nag me about drinking.

She was silent. She could feel his eyes on her but had no idea what he could be thinking.

– Why don't you go and see the priest again? You seemed happier for a while.

– No, Emma said savagely, then added – You've no respect.

You wouldn't talk in that way if you did.

He smiled.

– I worry about you, Harry, she mumbled, feeling as if she'd betrayed herself.

– Don't, he said lightly – you worry too much.

– Why did you marry her? What will you do with your life?

He shrugged, then said

– You're not well. Go back to bed for a bit and I'll make you some tea.

She didn't question him any more. Lying awake with the curtains drawn after he had gone out she felt a sense of humiliation. She had failed. All her life she had gone after one thing, and when she'd had to give up she had let herself transfer her ambitions onto him. She regretted it now, for she felt that if she hadn't tried so hard the failure wouldn't have been so bad. But there were things about him which had always surprised her. Even now she couldn't understand, why, when he had so obviously not wanted to wrestle, he had never actively resisted her plans for him. She thought perhaps that she'd tried to push him harder in an effort to make him resist and quarrel with her. She had nagged herself with obscure, morbid worries that he would never know what he wanted to do and just drift. She feared her own influence upon him most of all. During her 'bad time', when she'd done things that even then she hadn't liked to think about, her worst memory was a recurrent one, that of coming back to wherever they were staying and feeling his eyes upon her. Wondering how much he knew became an obsession with her, but she could never let a question past her lips. There was just his face; her reading of an implied reaction to what she'd done. He never rejected her. In a perverse, self-defeating way, she almost wished that he had. It would have meant he'd taken some step against going wrong, put himself away from her guilt. She remembered how three years ago she'd gone into a church and confessed a garbled, half-fictionalised account of something that she wanted to forget. The soothing feeling of absolution had been strangely undiminished by her awareness of her own hypocrisy. She had lit candles, she remembered, a whole bank of them blazing in white splendour and stood watching them burn down as if she found the flames fascinating, purifying. Now she put her hands over her face and groaned.

A slight noise disturbed her. She realised that perhaps she'd been asleep; the suddenness of her perception apparently coming after a long, blank interval. It was the sound of a footstep, very light, deliberately cautious. She placed it on the stair, then on the landing outside her door where it seemed to hesitate, or it might have been her own heartbeat drawing out the seconds. The step passed on, across to another door. Emma knew the architecture of the house's sounds, the creaks made by each door shutting against its frame. She identified it as Lucy's, with peculiar stealth. Emma counted on into the silence that followed the shutting of the door; five, ten, twenty. Moving quietly she got off the bed careful to open the door so it didn't squeak. She went across the landing, stepping instinctively where the boards were sound. The door to their room hadn't quite caught. Emma's fingers pushed it open, and through the widening crack she glimpsed Lucy standing by the basin and half the reflection of her face in the mirror as she raised something to her lips...

Emma moved quickly, powerfully, without thinking, and the tumbler shattered into splinters over the floor as she forced Lucy's hands away from her mouth. The bottle fell from stunned fingers, spilling red capsules as a strangled cry filled the air.

– Don't touch me!

Lucy wrenched herself free and sat down unsteadily in a chair. She put her hands over her face as if to shut out Emma before her. Emma leaned shakily on the basin, aware that her breath was coming faster than she liked.

– What possessed you? she said when she could. – Did you know what you were doing?

– It doesn't matter, said Lucy in a curiously quiet voice.

Emma bent down to pick up the pills from among the shards of glass. As she reached for the bottle and read the label she said

– Are these really vitamin pills?

Lucy gave a half startled laugh, then shrugged. – That's for you to find out it you want to. It doesn't matter any more.

Emma went out. Lucy heard the toilet flush several times. She put her hand up to her mouth as if she was going to be sick, then locked her fingers together in her lap, and stared at them. She smiled hopelessly, then her face changed. For a moment it was painfully alive, then she covered it with her hands as if only by shutting out could she accept the full knowledge of what she had become.

She looked up and saw Emma standing in the doorway.

–You don't recognise me, she burst out. – I've had your face before me in my dreams because you just stood there and watched and wouldn't help us. You saw what they did, she went on, but the passion had died out of her voice – it's such old history now it feels like it happened to someone else.

She got up and went across to the window. It was slightly open; she closed it automatically as drops of rain began to spatter the glass.

– I don't hold a grudge against you now. Who knows what might have happened. I was never sure about Nick, never able to convince myself that he really loved me after he persuaded me to steal the money. You might have done me a favour after all.

She laughed. – That money bought this house, didn't it? Strange to think, Emma watched her hands run along the sill – that this window frame, these bricks, came from that canvas bag I held between my hands.

– I didn't know you, Emma said after a long pause – why should I have helped you?

Lucy shrugged. – That's a brave answer. They're all dead apart from you. The boy was sick anyway, strange how things turn out. I killed George Ross; that wasn't so bad, not real; but the other one … he was laughing all the time, like he knew what I was going to do and didn't care, not till the last…

She shuddered and was quiet. – That horror was mine. I can't blame anyone else for it. I'd like to cut it out of myself, but it's part of me now, I can't.

– Did you plan to kill me? said Emma after a long pause.

– No, said Lucy heavily. – I would have hurt you through your son. But I found I couldn't hurt him, then I did, without wanting to.

She turned to face Emma.

– Tell me how much he knew, said Emma.

Lucy smiled faintly. – That depends how much he believed of what I told him.

– So you told him about me?

Lucy's face was suddenly distressed, almost frightened. – How could I tell what was going on inside his head? I'm asking you to help me, Emma. You're the last person I should ask but the only one I can.

– My son loves you.

Emma heard her own voice, remote.

– He shouldn't. He won't. I don't know what to do, Emma, she repeated.

She stood with her head bowed. As Emma stared at her, everything seemed to break down in confusion. She heard her own voice, stammering – You couldn't help it. You were driven to it. I'll help you. I'll protect you now.

Lucy said sadly – You might just be saying that to protect yourself. She turned back to the window and pressed her head against the pane.

– You can't leave him, said Emma at last. – He loves you. You wouldn't be that cruel.

– Emma, said Lucy's voice – has it occurred to you that he might not come back? That he might have just decided to go?

Emma was still. She ran the tip of her tongue round her lips without noticing, saying nothing.

Lucy was smiling desperately. – Emma, she said – what can I do?

The Kitty and Jenny Gang

One

I was running through the snow towards the central square. The leather soles of my new shoes skidded in the slush. As I ran, I kept looking behind me, but there was no pursuit.

The central square was lined with poplars. Eight streets radiated away. I came in on the west side, checked my pace. I needn't have bothered; there was no one around. The wooden skeletons of the stalls erected there in fine weather were heaped with snow. I placed my hand on one investigatively, drew it up covered with particles of ice.

A slight sizzling in the snow to my right caught my attention. Some flakes were landing on an exposed tram-line, which evaporated them in a fine plume of steam.

I walked towards the kiosk in the centre of the square where transport tickets were sold, and I pushed a note across the counter.

– Just give me as many as this will buy, I said, affecting a nonchalance I didn't feel. The woman in the kiosk looked at me for a moment. I had my head down and the collar of my coat was raised against the wind. Then she smiled and took the note. She wore fingerless gloves and the skin round her nails had changed colour with the cold. A tiny electric fire was visible behind her chair.

– These should keep you going for a couple of weeks.

She reached up to tug at a dispenser to the left of the counter. The tickets emerged as a strip; I heard the smooth electronic purr of the machine as the spool went round four times.

– Four hundred, she said.

I grabbed at the tangle of paper, shoved it into my pocket. She smiled at me faintly again.

– Careful, she said – you'll demagnetise them.

– Thanks, I said, and nodded before walking away.

The sides of the trams rose high and black, cut by a lighter line about two thirds of the way up, just below the windows. Their frames were polished imitation teak, contrasting with the lightweight alloys used elsewhere.

The snow blew in spasmodic flurries across the square. Only a few trams bore destination cards, which I gave up trying to read when I realised they were unfamiliar. I circled them warily, eventually picking one where I could see the conductor inside, reading his paper. I climbed the narrow steps at the back. He pushed a button to open the door, returning to his paper as soon as I was inside.

– Cold tonight.

I nodded.

– Be off in ten minutes.

I chose a seat near the front. The heating ran under the floor, relayed up from the electric tracks. I tried to rest my feet against the back of the seat in front, but they slipped off. The outside of the window was bleared with water, preventing me from seeing anything going on around me.

I realised that my limbs were trembling. The new shoes, that had cost me so much trouble, knocked together on the floor. I twisted round in my seat with some idea of looking for pursuit and caught the conductor's eye. He said

– Off soon.

Then came a slight hiss as the pneumatic door slid back in its groove, and the bus filled up quickly until all but a few seats were taken.

Someone squeezed in beside me. I rested my cheek against the window, instinctively turning away from casual contact.

Suddenly there was a dull battering outside. A white palm was splayed against the glass, blurring to and fro as it rapidly cleared an arc of water.

Then a face pressed up close. Alarm spread all along the tram as a row of faces appeared, squinting through the glass at the passengers inside.

I shrank back in my seat. Other people were fidgeting, standing up, and demanding some explanation from the conductor who'd abandoned his paper and was huddled up beside the rear door, apparently negotiating with someone outside.

The atmosphere was tense. When the first shock passed, voices became murmurs and eyes grew more active, flickering round at the unknown fellow passengers to speculate about the reason for the siege.

I sat tight. My neighbour cleared his throat twice. He put his hand up to his collar to loosen his tie. As he reached up, I could see a line where the edge of his cuff had chafed his wrist.

The door was released. I thought it would be more suspicious if I didn't turn around, so I followed the general craning. Suddenly I felt fingers on my arm. The man next to me tightened his grip.

– As I was saying, lad, he began in a voice that trembled in the stillness of the carriage.

Instantly all eyes turned back to him, and me. The officers coming up the aisle paused, then advanced more slowly.

– Sit up lad, for God's sake sit up, he begged me.

He was trembling.

I made an impatient movement to shake his grip and felt something hard against my ribs. The officers moved easily up on us. I stared at him with a feeling of disbelief. His mouth worked uncertainly, producing a bizarre quaver of anger that rose into a shriek.

– Leave me alone.

At the same moment his hand moved from against my ribs and there was a small quick sound like air escaping from a tyre. He dropped back on me, ultimately relaxed. I turned my head away as the police bent over him. They lifted his weight off me. There was not enough room to carry him down the aisle, so they dragged him.

The conductor came forward. His face was white and intensely sick. He stared at me.

– You all right?

I nodded. – You don't look too good yourself.

His arm brushed the back of the seat and he jumped back as if from something unclean. Then he recovered himself and tried to smile, but couldn't carry it through.

– You must have nerves of steel. Sure you wouldn't like to see a doctor?

I shook my head. – Who was he, anyway?

I'd found that in moments like this, if I pitched the first word right, I could force through the rest in a tone that went right against what I really felt.

The conductor's face became slightly aggrieved.

– McCarthy.

The people behind us caught the name and spread it swiftly down the tram. It obviously had associations I was unaware of.

The conductor was staring at me. I stumbled quickly to the next seat, aware that under his prolonged gaze a slight tic was developing at the corner of my mouth. He shook himself, and wandered back down the aisle, turning once to give me a look more indicative of disgust than suspicion. I put my hand up to my mouth, as if to cough, and bit my lip as hard as I could behind the cover of my fingers.

The bulb at the front of the tram began to flash. The conductor reached up to give the signal. The tram was off.

The lines ran far out beyond the city's boundaries. They had been constructed to ease an expansion that had never taken place. Along the unused roads, at dusk, lights shone out over the empty landscape.

I left the tram at a junction, unable to sit still any longer. Snow lay in deep drifts where it had been hastily swept aside. I looked up at the buildings that towered fifty or sixty storeys on either side of the broad street. At every level, swaying in the random gusts funnelled by the high walls, flexible pipes bridged the gap, cutting out all need to descend.

I was crossing another square when I heard a call. Instinctively I turned, registering shapes on the snow around a flicker of fire. When the call came again, I recognised my name, and went over.

– Hullo, Karl.

– Lorna.

I had been at school with her. She sat behind the fire,

55

sheltered by a tent made from three sheets of corrugated iron, absently feeding the flames with a piece of cardboard.

– How are you, Karl?

Something stirred behind her in the shelter. She smiled faintly and jerked her head back in its direction.

– That's June. Do you remember her?

I nodded.

– What is it, Lorna?

The voice was querulous, as if waking from a too heavy sleep.

– Karl.

– What's he doing here?

– What are you doing here, Karl?

I shrugged.

– Getting cold.

Lorna's laugh was thin. She made room for me to sit down. For a moment I held back, and the place was filled by June, who said

– Tell him to get lost.

Lorna let that pass. She kept looking at me, and her lips curved faintly.

– Going home, Karl?

I waited a little while before I said

– Just walking.

She nodded. June pushed herself up against her shoulder, extending one hand to the fire. She turned her head irritably aside, as if the flames hurt her.

– Tell him to go away.

She began to whine. Lorna's mouth twitched. I walked off.

Two

The snow did not let up. Towards morning, it turned to sleet, and as the air became a little warmer, I allowed myself to fall asleep in the doorway I'd occupied all night.

I was woken by someone shaking me. For some seconds I tried to resist, but there was no escape from the insistent hand.

– Come on, wake up. You are awake, she said as I groaned

in reply.

I sat up, rubbing my head. When I was able to focus, I saw she was a thin girl, light-haired, with pale eyes. She seemed surprised by what she saw.

– I was going to chuck you off. But you can come in, if you like.

I pulled myself up and followed her inside. We advanced along a passage. About halfway down, she stopped so suddenly that I ran into her.

– Careful.

She walked round me, brushing down my coat, then looked at my shoes.

– Did you steal them?

– Yes.

I returned her glance.

– You should get the right size next time.

She smiled at me warily and then her look became more serious.

– If anyone asks why you're here say Charlie Duck sent you.

– Duck? I repeated stupidly.

– Yes, Duck, she said, mimicking my tone. Then she set off down the passage again at a rapid pace. I called after her.

– Hey!

She stopped.

– What would he have sent me for?

She hovered for a moment, looking at me.

– Smile nicely, and you'll be alright. They won't ask you any deep questions.

– You might at least tell me your name.

I was feeling exasperated.

– I'm Alison, she replied. – We'd better hurry if you want some food.

As we passed through a panelled door at the end of the corridor, I heard the chink of cutlery. There was a table, set for four, of which two places were occupied.

The room was basically a square, with the corners rounded, so you couldn't tell quite where one wall ended and another began. The ceiling rose in a shallow dome. To a height of perhaps six feet, tanks lined the walls, beautifully engineered around the room's curves.

– Who's this, Alison?

– Duck sent him.

The woman at the head of the table turned her eyes to me.

– Where is Duck?

I just shook my head. The woman pushed aside her plate and bent forward, resting her chin on her heavily ringed hands.

– Charlie never knows what he's doing from one moment to the next, said Alison quickly.

– What is your name? The woman spoke across Alison. I was nervous and knew I showed it.

– Karl.

– O.K., Karl.

She smiled unexpectedly then reached for her plate again.

– Sit down. Since Duck sent you, you can have his place.

I obeyed. Alison passed a dish to me, and sat down herself. I ate voraciously, much to the amusement of the woman. Alison paid me no further attention. She sighed, fidgeting with her hair, then slowly crumbled a slice of bread. The man sitting across from her looked up. He caught the older woman's eye, wiped his lips, and said

– By the way, Audrey, Charlie may not show up for a couple of days.

The statement was delivered in a soft croak.

– Did he say something to you, James?

James gazed at her as if to acknowledge the lack of surprise her question gave him.

– Just a feeling I have, Audrey.

She shrugged. James reached for the coffee, filled his cup halfway and added three cubes of sugar. He stirred until, apparently, they were all dissolved, then turned to me for the first time.

– I can't drink this stuff anymore. But I think the smell is almost as good.

I nodded. His hair was white, brushed straight back from

his face, but he didn't look old. His skin was pale enough to be transparent: colour came and went very quickly making his face appear suffused with blood. I was relived when he turned away from me.

Audrey rose leisurely from the table, and disappeared through a door. Alison and I remained to watch James eat. He didn't say anything but I had the impression he enjoyed the audience. At last he wiped his lips and disappeared in turn.

I helped Alison clear up. She didn't speak to me. Then I was left alone.

For a while I walked back and forth, restlessly, in front of the tanks. Then I heard the quiet creak of a door and swung round to find that Alison had entered the room. She was smiling but looked worried.

– Sorry to abandon you, Karl, she said lightly as she crossed the room towards me. – Audrey says I'm to look after you.

She stopped about five feet away from me. When I moved a little nearer, she stepped back, as if anxious to preserve a prescribed distance.

– You won't mind staying here for a little while?

– Why not?

I copied her casual tone.

– But what happens when Duck gets back?

Her eyes shifted from me to the tank behind my head.

– I'll show you your room, she said quietly.

Realising I'd never get an answer, I followed her out.

Three

Audrey met us in the passage. In response to a slight movement of her head, Alison shrugged and walked away. Audrey gave me a grave smile, and we proceeded smoothly down the corridor.

She stopped in front of another of those panelled doors.

– Come in, Karl, she said, and opened it wide, ushering me in before her. Then she closed the door and indicated the further of the two chairs.

The room was small and square and had some heavy

textured paper on the walls. The armchair was comfortable. Audrey settled herself opposite me, folding her hands majestically to display her rings to the maximum advantage. She gazed at me thoughtfully as if waiting to hear my opinion on something.

– You're quiet.

I remained so.

– I'm not complaining, Karl. I prefer people to be quiet.

She bent forward so her rings caught the light, reflected from above on to a metal disc behind her. I could not help but look at them, as I was supposed to.

– What do you think?

– Very nice.

She laughed a short, dry laugh.

– Most people would think them beautiful.

– I can't tell. I'm colour-blind.

This seemed to amuse her greatly. She laughed for quite some time, stretching our her hands in front of her so the rings sparkled all the more. Then she wrapped her right fingers round her left and began to play with the bands, pushing them up and down over her knuckles in a way that kept my attention all the while her eyes were fixed on me.

– I don't think they're beautiful either, Karl.

I managed to raise my eyes to her face, which met me with a broad and kindly smile.

– They're power.

Her smile continued to widen. I felt curiously nerveless.

– Come on, Karl, don't look so shocked. I know Duck didn't send you. You're a better type than he usually picks.

Some kind of sigh escaped me. I was shaking my head.

– It's all right, Karl. I'm very glad you came.

I looked at her again. – Why?

– I think you could be useful.

She crossed her legs at the ankle and arranged a hand upon each knee.

– How? I said.

– That's for you to tell me. But if you are, she hesitated as if to emphasise what followed – you'll be quite safe here.

60

Her eyes were discreetly searching my face. I could see the trap she was leading me into, but somehow could not bring myself to resist it.

– You think I need to be safe? I said.

Her eyes underwent a subtle change. She straightened up a little and stared at me more directly.

– Why else did you come here?

I couldn't be sure that this wasn't a bluff. I didn't know in quite what way I was being tested. Her eyes met mine, held me for a long time. Eventually I said

– I stole a pair of shoes.

Her face relaxed a little, but otherwise did not alter its expression. She studied me gravely. When she next spoke her voice was appreciably softer.

– I want to show you something.

She took out a tiny key and slotted it into the wall, careful to shield the exact spot from my view.

I appreciated the delicacy with which she treated me now that I had given myself away. Sharing a little of her own secret would make me less likely to resent the hold she had over me. I was prepared to find whatever she showed me an illusion. She gave nothing away. She had me, and that was it.

– Come here, Karl.

A door had slid back in the wall. Again she made sure I went through in front of her. It was dark at first. She touched a switch and a steady light filled the place. I looked round, but could not see the source.

– Technology, Karl, she said, laughing at my bewilderment.
– Through here.

It was a large space, but I was not sure where the walls could be. Packing cases ranged up on every side, some battened down tight with the lead seals still intact, others half-open, with straw and shavings leaking out as if they'd been carelessly investigated.

I didn't think it worth the attempt to conceal my astonishment. I shrugged, and smiled at her, rather grudgingly.

– This is yours.

It had to be a statement, a question might have sounded

impertinent.

She nodded, with a half-smile that became melancholy as she gazed about her.

– Realisable assets.

I was genuinely intrigued. There was something monumental about it all.

– What are they?

She made a gesture with her hand that bordered on the theatrical.

– Jewellery. Antiques. Paintings. Coffee.

– Black market, I said, and nodded as if I'd begun to understand.

Her eyes narrowed, and she looked at me as if she was daring me not to be serious.

– The whole show, Karl, she said. – Everything.

There was a unique grandeur about the way she said this. I followed her automatically as she paced around.

– I measure myself by what's in this room, Karl. This is the hub. The nucleus.

I tried to quell the rising bitterness inside me. She ceased her pacing to stare at me with eyes that were infinitely sombre.

– Don't you approve, Karl?

I cast another look slowly round the room.

– It's just a little hard to take in, I said at last.

Four

I paused for a moment outside an open door.

James was inside. His back was turned to me. From where I stood I observed the regular sweep of his left arm, forwards and back, at a level slightly above his waist.

He was ironing a shirt. I pushed the door gently with the back of my hand, extending my fingers so it glided inwards with very little sound.

I didn't step inside. I wasn't sure whether he knew I was there. Studying his back closely, I was impressed by how relaxed he looked. He varied the strokes of the iron quickly and precisely. In a moment he'd finished and turned round.

Seeing me, he laid the shirt carefully on the back of a chair and came over to the door.

For a second he didn't say anything, just looked me up and down. There was a curious excitement about him that I couldn't place.

– Have you been talking to my sister?

– Your...?

His laugh was a very strange sound.

– You're going to stay here, then?

– For a while.

– Good. That's very good.

Behind the slightly detached stare it seemed a number of expressions were continually at play.

I nodded. He seemed to smile without moving his mouth.

– Come in, Karl.

I teased myself by detecting an echo of Audrey's intonation. His collar was pulled a little higher than most men wear them, and for the first time I wondered if the soft insidious croak was the result of some neck injury.

– Why did you accept her invitation?

His measured tone may not have been calculated to rile me. He leaned back and lightly touched the shirt that lay across the chair.

– It is your business.

He didn't reply to that. My gaze went round the room, rested on a silver-coloured shallow box that lay on the table.

– It's for cigarettes.

I looked up.

– A souvenir.

His mouth quivered with suppressed laughter. After a second I found myself joining in.

The room rang with the sound. I'd never laughed like this before. Gradually I found myself weak with giddy hiccoughs.

James had stopped some time before. He stood regarding me with a tolerant amused smile.

– It gets rather dull here. If you like to read I have some books.

The laughter in me died with a final splutter. He beckoned

me to the far side of the room. There were five shelves built into the wall, jammed solid with yellow spines.

– Westerns, he said.

I must have looked blank.

– If you don't like to read, he said, ushering me back to the centre of the room – there are other ways to pass the time. The fish are very soothing, he continued mildly. – I can watch them for hours.

He turned an almost beneficent gaze on me.

– They all have their ways, he said.

Five

The next time we all met was at supper.

I had been sitting in the room assigned to me, which bore marks of having been cleared out in a hurry. At the back of the mirror lay a comb, to which a few hairs still clung. Charlie's, I guessed.

There was something a little eerie about the place. I sat on the freshly turned-down bed. When the springs creaked, I thought of how they must have shifted under his weight a few nights ago.

I began to search the room, feeling the walls for hidden cupboards, running my finger along where the carpet went against the wall. It was really to reassure myself that there was nothing of his here. Then I passed into the bathroom which boasted smooth grey walls. I was giving up in relief when the door of a cupboard suddenly clicked back, and I was confronted by a large dark bottle, unlabelled.

I unscrewed it, and dabbed a little of the contents on my tongue. It stung slightly, very sweet. Quickly I replaced the top and let the cupboard shut just as a light rap sounded from the outer door, as if someone had knocked their knuckles against it in passing.

There was no one in the corridor. Rather self-consciously I smoothed my clothes, which were stained where the snow had melted repeatedly. I looked at my shoes, licked my finger, and rubbed away some of the white powder that had formed on the surface of the new leather. I shrank from using the comb, but after I'd washed it it was alright. Catching myself in the mirror gave me another uneasy moment. My hands became very awkward as I thought of the different reflection the mirror would have cast just a few evenings before.

I had been in no state earlier to appreciate the formal perfection of that room. As I paused on the threshold, and saw their heads turn towards me, I quelled the uneasy restlessness that had earlier threatened to overwhelm me, and with an instinctive smile, found myself crossing a vast area of floor. A soft artificial light permeated the room, again from no visible source, though as I gazed up past the tanks, it seemed strongest on the silvery-coloured shutters occurring at intervals high in the walls. My feet made no noise on the floor, which had the slight spring of cork.

As I neared the table Alison got up and returned in a moment carrying a tray. She put plates down at each place in turn, subtly varying the way they made contact with the cloth. James' came down very gently, Audrey's with restrained force, and mine with equivocation. I glanced at her, but her face was stony. Audrey smiled and poured me some water.

– I hope everything's comfortable, Karl.

There was a bewildering ease in her manner. She kept smiling at me while Alison was dishing up the food. The atmosphere of the meal was so oddly civilised that I found myself, contrary to inclination, talking smoothly and rapidly. Audrey listened, and was flatteringly amused. James laughed at odd intervals, but seemed more interested in his food. I listened to my voice going on and on, watching my hand playing with the fork on my plate. Occasionally I would pause, and lift the fork to my mouth, but I hardly tasted what I chewed.

Alison cleared the plates away and brought in the coffee. James repeated his ritual of the morning: I let mine cool in the cup without tasting. Audrey blew on hers ferociously, drained it quickly, and took some more. The clink of the spoon against fine china as she stirred in a swirl of cream reawakened my attention. I glanced at the girl next to me. She hadn't bothered with her cup. I felt sympathy but was unable to express it. Looking up, I found James' eyes on me and felt exposed.

– No more news about Charlie, said Audrey lightly.

James' gaze was quickly transferred. Momentarily I followed it, then dropped my eyes to stare hard at the table, feeling that the less I knew of this the better. Audrey must have noted my move, for she altered her tone to deliberately include us all.

– It is a bit odd him not coming back. James, Alison, don't you think so? Of course Karl doesn't know Charlie – but it's not the behaviour you'd really expect of an old friend.

There was a living silence. Alison's hand crawled on the table-cloth. I froze my muscles, fearing the slightest move that could be construed as a response.

– Well, said Audrey, after her eyes had rested deeply on us each in turn. – I never really got on with him myself. I expect we all feel that way. James, Alison?

Her voice trailed away with this playful interrogation.

From the corner of my eye I saw Alison's fingers stretch out over the cloth with an intentness that betrayed she'd really wanted to gather them into a fist.

From across the table came a slight gasp. I looked up and there was James laughing without a sound.

– You've got it wrong, Audrey, he said.

If it were possible, Alison tensed a little more beside me. Audrey threw her a quick glance, then stared at her brother, who met her gaze with a laugh that caused her eyes to harden and narrow.

– Have I, James?

She emphasised each word.

– Yes, Audrey.

While she watched him he pushed back his chair a little and crossed his legs.

– Charlie'll be coming back, he reasserted.

Audrey's face was like fire.

– I don't suppose you know when?

– Soon, said James, and chuckled. He pushed the chair a

little further, and leaned right back.

Audrey got up and left the room. After swinging back and forward for a moment, and with a sidelong glance at us, James followed her.

Alison let out a long breath. When I turned to her she looked away from me almost angrily. She put her hands up to her face, moving her head slowly from side to side as if trying to clear a pain. When I realised she was crying I felt worse. and remained in my chair, making a too conscious effort not to look at her.

It didn't last long. She sat up and wiped her eyes, even giving me a strained smile.

– What is it? I asked, well aware that I was presuming too much on her appearance of recovery. My voice sounded dry and harsh. I should have left her alone, but some instinct demanded that I ask her.

She gave me a disgusted look, which hurt because I deserved it. Then she checked herself, and replied in a voice as flat as my own.

– Charlie took some money with him.

I nodded. Suddenly she leaned forward, eyes strangely lit by the knowledge of what she had to impart.

– James noticed the money was missing.

For a moment I was confused. The emphasis struck me as wrong. Then I realised what she meant and leaned forward until our heads were very close.

– James doesn't care about money, she breathed.

I gazed into her eyes. There were questions that could not be asked between us. She seemed to grow shy and after a moment, drew back.

– Come and look at the fish, she said.

I followed her to the nearest tank. She cleared her throat and started to tell me the names of some of its inhabitants. I felt myself smile. She turned away from the glass, and fixed me with pleading seriousness. Then she spoke, and her voice was at variance.

– Do you know, she said, and laughed. – I've sometimes had the strangest feeling they're looking at me.

She lightly touched my arm. I heard a noise and turned to see James coming back into the room. The girl walked quickly over. As I followed I found the way she moved disturbed me.

– Is it all right? she said in a tone of utter naturalness.

He gave her a look of intelligence and smiled at me.

– Perfectly, he said, addressing her. He had something in his hand that he was playing with. Noticing my stare, he held up the cigarette box.

– Souvenir.

Alison laughed too. I hung back a little, conscious of a desire to find that laugh forced. James glanced from me to her in the same quick, conspiratorial way.

– He still finds it a bit strange here.

She took his arm, gave him a subdued and mysterious smile. His gaze lingered on her. Then he turned to me with a deliberately careless air. Reluctantly I took my eyes away from her fingers on his arm.

– Isn't she beautiful?

It was delivered as an open drawl. His face was watchful for my reply. I nodded, with what I judged to be respectful appreciation. Alison froze beside him, mute, her face intent on registering nothing. There was a slight relaxation. As he looked at her, nervousness was smoothed out into a smile.

– He finds you beautiful, he said.

Her fingers must have tightened on his arm. She kept that smile, though with her eyes lowered. There was something not quite expected in his look: a curiosity blended with the happy menace with which this was put.

– I –

He touched her shoulder gently.

She seemed to subside at this, raising her eyes. His face was intent on her, as if she were a stranger. I'd flinched when he touched her. Now I felt I should turn away, but couldn't. He pulled her lightly towards him, and she responded with a neat almost doll-like motion. Then they moved quickly out of the room, and I was left looking after them.

Six

An absolute silence descended on the room. Lights were dimmed. There was a sudden flurry of activity in the tanks. Fish scales glowed through the water.

For a moment I found myself staring stupidly at the long stream of bubbles rising through a corner of the tank. On impulse I jabbed my finger at the glass. A couple of their heads came up against it on the other side. I really disliked their faces, and jabbed the glass again, more viciously, in the hope of introducing some slight tremor into their perfectly ordered world. I jolted my finger a bit, that was all, and as I turned away was conscious of the muscle tension changing in my face, though whether I was supposed to cry or laugh I didn't know.

The room held no mirrors, for which I was grateful: the half-image reflected from the surface of the tanks was disconcerting enough. I felt a sort of shaking in my limbs, and let myself slide to the floor, sitting cross-legged in a heap just below the level of the glass. From there I was squinting up at the underbellies of the fish, through phosphorescence exuded by a few rocks, partly concealed by plants, whose stems seemed constantly in motion through the strange light.

I was transfixed by the hypnotic rhythm, and felt a choking tension in my throat. When I put my hands up round my neck, experimentally squeezing to relieve this pressure, I found it had ebbed away, and was left with a great sense of tiredness that also threatened to desert me if I did not obey it, and leave me with that sadness from which sleep would supply at least a temporary relief. I curled up like an animal, and dreamed of nothing.

Alison woke me again. I felt her hand on my shoulder, and rolling over, grasped it within my own.

– Karl. What are you doing here?

There was a soft outlet of breath. She put her other hand over mine, perhaps working gently to free her own, but after a moment she was still. My hand grew warm enclosed in hers. I listened to her breathing, stared up at the pupils of her eyes shining faintly in the dark.

– What are you thinking about?

I was surprised by my new, almost jealous tone. As she moved her head slightly, the light caught the curve of her cheek and outlined the tiny hairs that clustered close to the skin.

– It's my habit not to think.

She was sad too. She had been with him.

Gradually I levered myself up from the floor until I was sitting beside her. She didn't move. She seemed sunk in some contemplation of her own. I was filled with a protective tenderness. When she sighed, I felt it within myself.

– Alison, I said, and hardly recognised my voice, which came as a whisper in the quiet. – Come away with me.

At first I thought she hadn't heard, then she turned and mouthed some words that I struggled to read. I looked at her, feeling the blank incomprehension on my face, and she moved her eyes slightly, I thought reluctantly, to imply a negative. My face pleaded. Her eyes were very wide, seeming luminous, as she shook her head.

Barely realising, I'd moved nearer, and now my lips formed the words – Why not? She extended her hands to my face as if to push me back a little. I brushed her palm with my lips in passing and our eyes held in a serious and very sad look which seemed to last until there was nothing of us left.

– Alison, I said, and my voice sounded ugly and thick.
– Please come away. You're not happy here.

– Oh, Karl, what a reason.

Her voice was level. She shifted, until kneeling, she was a little taller than me. Her expression flickered, but was controlled. I could see that she pitied me. My voice ground out in appalling contrast to her calm replies.

– You love James, then.

She was beginning to get angry.

– Don't you?

She slapped me hard across the cheek. Then she took my hands and kissed them, I stared up at her stupidly. She stroked my hair. Her eyes were concerned, slightly ashamed.

– I hope no one heard that.

I struggled upright. She squatted back on her heels and put her arms round my neck.

– I'm sorry I brought you here.

– I wouldn't have met you, I said, with a self-conscious, almost hysterical laugh.

She surveyed me gravely.

– I chose to stay, I said defensively.

She sighed and held me a little tighter.

– You don't have to, surely. You should leave while you can.

Her eyes searched mine. Then she said

– What did Audrey say to you?

– Nothing really.

Her arms remained round my neck, but her face changed.

– Won't you tell me, Karl?

– Nothing!

She stood up, and pulled me up with her.

– Poor Karl. You're stuck here then.

Her lips twitched slightly. I was aware of having make a mistake.

– Would it make a difference if I wasn't? I said lamely, striving to inject conviction into my tone.

She stiffened slightly under my touch, and I went cold.

– It's you that keeps me here, I said desperately. She laughed, a distressed sound, harsh and short.

It sounded remote. I pushed her away and fled.

Seven

– Hullo, Karl.

I edged into his room. The table was spread with a cloth covered with metal parts which shone in the intense light of the lamp suspended above them.

James took up one piece at a time to examine it. He had not rolled up his sleeves, but bands held them in place just below the elbow. Under his breath he whistled something I couldn't recognise.

– Alison said you couldn't sleep.

He turned to me with one of the metal bits still in his hand, gripping through a soft cloth, with which he languorously polished it.

– Yes, I said. – I think I was too tired.

He nodded, and turned back to take up another piece.

– It's always hard, the first night in a new place.

I lingered a while, taking pleasure in his neat manipulation of each object. He seemed to like me watching. Jealousy was out of place; the events of last night seemed faintly ludicrous now.

– Have you any experience with guns?

I shook my head.

– Come and look.

I ventured over obediently. Before my eyes the weapon was swiftly assembled. I felt excited. He cast a sidelong glance, and pushed it in my direction.

– How's your co-ordination?

– Pretty good.

He nodded. – Pick it up.

I balanced it carefully on the fleshy pad between thumb and forefinger. He made a slight sound of displeasure, and closed his hand over mine, readjusting all my fingers. When he took his hand away I was holding it correctly, experiencing all sorts of strain on tiny muscles I'd never used.

– Keep it steady.

I moved my head a little to one side so I could look along the barrel. James was packing the cloth away behind me; I could hear the swift movements as he shook and folded it before stowing it in a drawer. Then there was the sound of a tap running, and the steady soaping of hands. I shifted my feet a little, conscious of an unaccustomed ache in my shoulder.

There were quick footsteps outside the door, and Alison came in. My fingers gave way quite suddenly, and the gun fell to the floor. James turned in irritation as I stooped to pick it up, and faced him, white and shaking.

Alison was saying quickly in a low voice

– It was my fault. I startled him.

The blood drained from James' face and returned. Soap

had spattered the front of his shirt. I was stammering that it was my fault. He made a gesture to cut us both short and retrieved the gun from my hand. Quickly checking it, he laid it on the table and waved us out.

When he'd shut the door behind us I felt Alison's hand on my arm. She said quickly

– Charlie's come back.

It took me a moment to work out. I looked down at her hand. She removed it self-consciously and said

– You'll be careful.

Her voice was serious and rather flat.

– I have to get some things. He's in there with Audrey. Go on in.

She touched my arm lightly to emphasise the command. I anticipated some sort of reaction to her touch, but was unable to work out what I was feeling towards her.

– Be careful, Karl, she repeated, giving me a light push towards the door which I opened without further preparation.

What I saw came as a shock to me. For a moment I just stared stupidly at Audrey, sitting very upright in a chair, and the man at her feet sobbing, with his face buried in her lap.

Audrey's eyes met mine gravely.

– He's had a lot to drink.

I concentrated on closing the door very gently behind me. Then I ventured a little nearer. I wanted to stay where I was, but thought it would not be politic.

– I hope you passed a pleasant night, Karl, she said. – This is Charlie, who you've heard us all talk about.

In response to a nod of her head, I dragged my feet a little faster across the vast area of floor. Something in my face was unsatisfactory, she gave me an irritated glance and stared down at Charlie's head, tightening her lips.

The door banged to behind me, and Alison stepped past, carrying a bottle and glass which she put down when she reached him. She exchanged a look with Audrey, who nodded. Alison stooped down behind him and put her hands under his armpits to peel him off. Audrey stared impatiently in my direction, but by the time I'd reached them Alison had him propped against the leg of the chair and was pouring, with rather unsteady hands, a large measure into the glass from the bottle. She produced a handkerchief to wipe his face but he thrashed around under her touch and nearly upset the glass.

Audrey got up from the chair and stood a little distance away, her back turned.

– You won't sober him by giving him more drink.

– I can't let James see him like this.

Their eyes met, and as quickly looked away.

Alison muttered something, and bent over the recumbent man. I was looking at the soles of her shoes, and then Audrey tapped me on the arm and led me to another part of the room. Moving like a sleepwalker, I heard my voice thickly ask a question.

– Why has Charlie come back? What's going to happen to him?

– Why not ask him? He can still answer you.

When the door opened again she swung me round, placing her hands over my ears so I heard only a muffled shot.

Incidents on the Road

Police block

It was as if I'd been exposed to an electric shock. All the revulsion I'd felt for my job over the past months welled up at once and I started to walk towards the door, past the whining machines beneath the bright light and the figures bowed above them, transfixed by the continual rattle of coins.

– Where are you going, Judy?

– Piss off.

She flushed and stepped across me to bar my way. I stood there, mute, and glowered at her. She regained her calm, and spoke steadily;

– Not with those things.

My fingers seemed very large as I fumbled with the knots that held the overall in place. Her face was still. As knots unravelled, the rolls of money dug into my stomach. I pulled the garment over my head and used my arm as a spindle, closing the money within a tight roll of cloth in a gesture that became increasingly futile as I sensed the smile spreading across her face.

– Judy!

I tossed the roll at the ground where it struck her ankle, and brushed past out into the salt air, following the line of the wooden planks until I'd quit the pier and was heading along the esplanade, between the sea and the afternoon traffic. It was hot and I began to sweat. As I slowed, the wind off the sea caught me, and my clothes felt like ice.

A car pulled up. I glanced at it involuntarily and caught the eye of the woman leaning across as if to ask me directions.

Her eyes were watery and bloodshot. She had reddish hair and pale skin that looked firm and healthy. I found myself saying

– I'll show you,

and saw her hand move to unlock the door, smiling as I opened it and slipped inside.

– This is very kind of you, she said as the car pulled away from the kerb. I wriggled slightly in my seat. The overheated upholstery was sticking to the back of my legs.

– Can you put on the seat-belt, she said, taking one hand from the wheel to indicate it – in case we get stopped.

I bent forward, and stole a glance up at her. A private smile played around her lips, which were pale and dry, giving the impression they had not enough skin. Her chin was sharp, but blurred by a suggestion of fat.

– There are some cigarettes in there.

I took the hint, lit one, and passed it over. She held it gingerly, inhaled deeply, and coughed. Then she opened the window and threw it out. I found a packet of pastilles in the glove compartment and passed her one. She sucked noisily for a second, then spat it out.

– Thanks, she said. Her cough had gone.

She changed gear as we turned off the coast road and headed uphill. I leaned back in my seat: the cold wind ventilating the car made it quite pleasant. I smoothed my clothes and undid the top button of my blouse, scraped my hair up from my neck and let it fan out over the back of the seat. Then I teased off one shoe with the toe of the other, rotating my heel to study the clinging patch where a blister had burst against the dark nylon.

– Why don't you take your gloves off?

I laughed out loud and glanced down at my hands encased in black cotton. Looking up again, I caught her eye. She shook her head and smiled a bit, then turned away.

– It was part of my job, I said, fumbling with words for what already seemed remote. Staring down at my hands as if I couldn't quite believe in them, I laughed again, rather oddly.

– What was your job?

– Changing people's money in the arcade so they could lose it in the games machines.

– Sounds terrible.

I gestured self-consciously. Without removing her eyes

from the road she gave me another quick smile, and pulled across into a different lane. Idly I raised my hands, then lowered them.

There was activity up ahead. The traffic had come to a halt, and there were lights across the road, blinking ineffectually against the glare of the sun setting over in the west. They cast weak shadows upwards, elongating the trees at the roadside so they threatened to close over. I rolled down the window and stuck out my head to look along the column of cars. There was a restless movement next to me as she drummed at the steering wheel with her fingers.

– There's a man coming. A policeman.

She raised her shoulders indifferently and sighed.

– There must have been an accident.

He went to her side of the car, asked for her licence. She handed it over with a flippant gesture. He straightened up, and studied it for some time before passing it back.

– What's wrong with it?

His face showed that he resented her tone. He glanced from her to the car and back.

– There's been a murder.

It barely showed but he succeeded in rattling her.

– Two young women had their throats cut in the North Wood.

– That's the other side of town, I interposed, leaning across her. – Why are you stopping people here?

– We've got men on all the roads.

As my gaze met his, he looked irritated, insecure. Then he turned and walked back along the column, his shadow brushing up against the cars.

– You all right? I asked the woman. She shrugged impatiently. I put my gloved hand on hers where it rested on the wheel, lightly touching all her fingers. After a second she removed it and didn't look at me.

The policeman returned with another, older man. I could see them arguing as they came along.

– Sorry to bother you, girls.

She passed a hand across her forehead.

77

– What's the matter, officer?

He gave her a warily sympathetic look, then glanced at his colleague, who stubbornly resisted the glance and addressed himself to us.

– Someone described a car like yours parked near the wood.

The woman raised her head and spoke scathingly.

– You mean someone said they saw a black car. There are thousands.

He looked as if he might have shrugged.

– The description was more specific than that.

There was a moment of silence.

– Are you going to arrest me? she asked softly.

Her eyes flickered from one to the other. I stirred in my seat, disconcerted by the directness of her challenge.

The older man cleared his throat, and addressed me.

– Perhaps you can tell us something about yourselves.

– We came down from London this morning.

I glanced at her as if for corroboration. – We were going to drive along the coast, then find somewhere to stay.

– What's your name?

– Judy Smith.

As I met his glance, he gave me a tired smile.

– All right, girls. We shouldn't keep you much longer.

I watched him walk to the head of the column. The younger man had gone to check on the cars behind us.

She signed and scratched her head.

– I don't like the police.

It was practically dark in the car, and the shadowed outline of her face made me feel somehow peaceful. I let myself stretch out as far as the seat allowed. A gratifying, almost titillating exhaustion spread through my limbs.

– What's your name? I said on the verge of a yawn.

– Laura.

River

We drove for most of the night. Slight changes in the engine's

78

pitch made me aware, in my semi-conscious state, where the road varied. Sometimes I raised myself to look as a white wall flashed by.

Just before dawn we pulled on to a rough track, then slithered across grass. Something brushed the roof of the car as we came to a halt.

I must have slept again for when I woke it was light. Laura was doing something at the front of the car. For a moment I lay still, eyes half-closed, to listen to the faint sounds she made. Then I stretched my neck tentatively, and my limbs, one by one until cramp receded and I opened the door and got out.

We were parked underneath a tree. On either side the boughs bent down gently to cloak us, creating a barrier of leaves through which the diffused light shone green. I walked to the edge of the circle and ran my arms up along the branches until a satisfying coolness drenched my clothes and the scent of the leaves made me giddy.

– Feel better?

I turned. She was standing behind me. There was a smear of oil on her left cheek and her eyes were barely open.

– You should have woken me if you wanted help.

She smiled and shook her head.

– You must have been tireder than I was.

Her tone was friendly, but there was a slight reserve which might have been due to exhaustion. I stepped back a little and looked around.

– Why here?

She shrugged.

– I don't like to park too near the road. You get people coming along.

– How did you find your way in the dark?

She gave me a guarded smile and said

– You don't have to bother about that, Judy.

She turned quickly, leaving me at a loss, and walked back to the car, her light shoes making little sound. The green shadows gave everything an eerie tint. Slowly I rolled up my wet sleeves. My forearms glowed as I parted the curtain of leaves and stepped outside.

We were on the bank of the river. The sun was still low in the sky but the last traces of mist were already dispelling. My feet sank into sodden grass. I tried to gauge the time from the sun's position and let my failure yield to a sense of pleasant aimlessness. Any noises I could hear were much too faint to provide a clue.

I studied my surroundings with passive deliberation, gaining such satisfaction from the way I moved that I felt the desire to do something extravagant fill me with a slow excitement that was hard to contain. The field behind me was empty, the road invisible.

On the opposite bank rushes grew close to the water. I stared at the coal-black mud, castellated by the river's progress. Its current was hard to discern: just a few faint ripples indicated a tug towards the far bank. My head turned to look along. The river became a flat stretch of grey, running straight where the bank had been improved. Then a smudge of trees, and it vanished, curving slowly beyond my sight.

I took off my clothes and slipped into the cold water. Its first shock forced the air from my lungs, then I kicked out strongly, loving the feeling of moving through water the sun had not yet begun to warm. It had a silky texture that would be unbearable later in the day. I hadn't felt so good in a long time. My legs and arms pumped through the water in perfect tune.

– Oh, Laura, this is marvellous! Come in.

She was standing on the bank with her arms crossed, watching me. Her presence made my satisfaction a little more deliberate. I kicked out my legs in a mighty splash, conscious of a desire to tease her, and saw her flinch as a few drops of water fell dangerously near in the sunlight.

– I'll teach you to swim, I persisted, generous in the sense of my advantage.

As she shook her head the sun caught her face and the furrow between her brows.

– I think you can drown enough for both of us.

I laughed. As I heaved round on my stomach to tread water,

her expression took on a complexity that puzzled me.

– Let's get on our way. Can you drive?

I nodded. As I climbed up the bank she looked at me with a glance in which amusement mingled with something else.

– Where are we going?

She made a casual gesture. – I've got some stuff stored in a place a few miles from here.

– And then?

I was drying my feet with excessive care. As I straightened up it was as if her eyes had moved away from me rather sharply.

– Oh. Her manner was offhand. – Anywhere you like.

I donned my clothes soberly, feeling slightly ashamed of playing her up. As I walked with her back to the car her expression was warm but brittle. She was more nervous than I had suspected or perhaps tiredness exaggerated her reactions.

I really liked her. She was tricky, which I appreciated, and made me less worried about being moody myself. She had a car, and wherever I might end up it was better than stewing on the pier all summer.

House

It was a long time since I had handled a car, and I experienced a steady, if rather remote, excitement as the road smoothly disappeared before me. Laura dozed in the passenger seat, her chin pressed right down against her neck. Occasionally a stifled snore escaped her. When this happened I would glance across, and moving my eyes back, would catch an almost conspiratorial look in the mirror. Her hands lay limply in her lap. A slight swell of fat at the wrist was swiftly contained by buttoned cuffs which had that shiny look clothes get when they've been worn too long.

She opened her eyes with difficulty and sat up.

– What is it? she asked, seeing me grin.

– You, I said truthfully.

She wasn't quite sure she liked that.

– What about me?

I smiled and shook my head, devoting exaggerated care to the tension of the wheel between my hands.

We turned down a lane that rapidly petered out into a track. I had a dim glimpse of a pond, overhung by trees. When Laura put her hand on the wheel, I braked a little too quickly and turned to her. She smiled.

– Do you want to come?

– Your stuff's here?

She raised her eyebrows at my surprise and slipped out of the car. She walked ahead with a slightly floundering motion, dipping and jerking to avoid the deposits of mud that lingered though there'd been no rain for a week. Mosquitoes and flies swarmed around us; I kept my hand up in front of my face to swat them away.

We came level with a broken paling. She stopped.

– Here? I echoed.

She bent her shoulder to lift a gate which hadn't been disturbed for a while. I followed her through onto a path that led up to a house of incredible decrepitude.

– I used to live here, she said, as if needing to explain.

It was all right inside, which worried me, because I felt that when it started to crumble it would do so very quickly. I followed her through the rooms, fitting my footsteps to her own in the obscure hope of minimising disturbance.

– I was here as a child, she said. – My parents moved to London when I was eight.

– I would have been relieved.

A sideways smile suggested my desire to leave had reinforced her need to talk. She went on apologetically.

– I hated moving. As soon as we got to London my cat ran away.

For a moment she fidgeted uneasily.

– I'm sure she came back here. I wanted to come and look but they wouldn't let me.

Her voice went very small. I gingerly avoided leaning back against a door.

– It was only a cat, Laura, I said, trying to comfort without feeling any sympathy.

Silence ensued. A nervous desire to laugh was tempered by vague horror as I stood there looking at her in the almost ruined house.

At last she sighed very quietly and said

– My stuff's in here.

Two suitcases and a grip, which she wiped casually before handing me the larger case. Without further words we left the house. I wasn't tempted to look back and don't know whether she was.

Café

We were sitting together in a café drinking ice cream sodas. Being Saturday morning, it was full of prospective teenage couples who made me self-conscious. Laura, who was either oblivious or better at concealing her reactions than I, was gurgling with her straw at the last pink fragments. After a couple of sips at mine, I stirred it aimlessly, wishing I'd held out for a cup of coffee. I was impatient for Laura to finish but as she showed no signs of hurrying I picked up the paper a previous customer had left and glanced at it.

– Look, I said to Laura – about those girls who were killed.

I folded the paper appropriately and passed it across. A slight frown creased her brows as she read, then shoved it back to me.

– So they caught someone.

– Seems so.

She shrugged. – Can I have your soda?

I passed it across without a word, watched with amusement as she meticulously replaced my straw with her own.

– I keep expecting you to say you used to come here when you were fourteen.

– Oh but I did, she said, in such a way that I was unable to tell whether she was joking.

I plaited my fingers together on the table and leaned forward.

– Do you often revisit your past?

83

She sucked up the last of the soda appreciatively and raised her head.

– Judy, she said with great solemnity – it's in your honour.

We looked at each other, and simultaneously faltered. Her tone was so close to mockery that for a moment we both doubted whether it was. She cast down her eyes and fiddled with her glass, but her composure was gone. I craned round the room with such a start I found it hard to believe we hadn't both become instantly noticeable.

– I do like you, Judy.

She spoke from just above the rim of the glass. I hardly dared reply or look at her.

– In all sorts of ways.

This time she looked up and met my gaze with a disconcerting smile. I found something very sweet in her voice and was conscious of a desire to prolong all the implications of that moment.

If this showed on my face it made her laugh.

– Judy, she said – let's go.

She pushed some coins beneath her saucer and abstracted the two straws with a sleight of hand I was expected to see. Then another smile, kinder because less challenging, and possessed of a gravity I'd have found it hard to assume.

– Judy, she said again.

In some obscure way I'd already lost out. A flicker of concern across her face betrayed the panic I'd let show in mine.

– Laura, I...

It was all bewilderingly clear. There was a hint of tenderness in her smile. I passed out of the café with the strongest commitment to something I knew nothing about.

The Bridge

We went into a shop to buy provisions for our journey. Laura selected biscuits and several cartons of fruit juice. While I half-heartedly added a loaf, Laura took jam and a sheaf of chocolate bars. She paid with a large note and I found myself carrying the bags. Laura walked slightly ahead, whistling thoughtfully and twirling the bunch of keys round one finger.

– It's too hot to drive now, she called back at me. – What do you say we dump this stuff in the car and set off this evening?

She gave me a slightly teasing smile as if to indicate what a good idea this was. I smiled agreement – it was her car, after all.

We reached the entrance of the underground car park. There were narrow concrete steps at one side for pedestrians, but Laura ignored them in favour of the ramps the cars went down, seeming careless of any danger we might incur. She took the bag from me and swung it as she walked with a slight swagger down the middle of each slope through the chilly petrol-saturated gloom.

We put the stuff in the back, beside her luggage. As she was locking up, I was taken by a feeling of awkwardness, partly sad and partly reckless, as if I didn't really know what to do but was being overtaken by events against my will. Staring at her back outlined by the coat in the flickering light I had a confused impulse towards her, in which an almost violent tenderness was dominated by something else that made no sense to me. Turning, she smiled at me thoughtfully, and taking my arm, led me up the steps into the sunlight.

– What would you like, Judy?

– Somewhere quiet.

She rubbed her free hand across her face as if tired or trying to think. For some reason this aroused my suspicion, and I gave her a quick mulish glare which she evaded, seeming about to say something sharp, then changing her mind.

– I don't really know my way round here.

– Neither do I.

We looked at each other, then smiled.

– Let's wander.

She took my hand and squeezed it lightly. I looked down on her fingers which were white and slightly plump. We both seemed to have recovered our good humour. As we walked along, we responded to a sense of complicity which took the form of throwing a mystery round ourselves, emphasising our behaviour in peculiar ways and engineering a private joke that permitted us to laugh at everything around us. We covered the main streets in this way, but when we came into the quieter suburbs we were more subdued, and strolled in silence along the tree-lined streets, occasionally glancing at each other, but mostly self-contained, soaking up the dull warmth of the afternoon.

– Look Laura, I said suddenly – there's a bridge.

It poked up a little oddly behind the houses. She gave me a look as if she was trying not to laugh at me. I grew self-conscious, and stopped.

– Come on, she said – let's look at your old bridge.

It was at the end of the street. She took my arm again and led me on. She seemed amused with the whole thing. I didn't like her being amused with me, but it would be worse if I demurred.

We climbed a flight of iron steps, then lolled against the sides of the walkway that spanned the tracks and platforms of a station. She peered over the edge, and I looked at her. As a train pulled in underneath she raised herself on her toes with a slight exclamation of surprise.

– It's hot, Judy.

I made my face as nonchalant as I could manage and she gave me a look perhaps intended for mystification. I followed her across the bridge, listening to the slightly mannered taps her shoes gave out against the iron.

At the bottom of the steps a narrow lane ran straight along beside a high wall. From the bridge I'd glimpsed trees and thought it was a park, but when we found the gate and entered, it was a graveyard.

– Put on your gloves, Judy, Laura murmured. – And be a young widow. I'll support you.

We proceeded in that way. The place was overgrown, with the thick foliage of early summer already wilted by the scorching heat. But the paths had been freshly cleared, so the clipped-back bushes presented a vivid uniform wall of green, and the impression was rather that of a well-maintained maze than a cemetery. It was a place for assignations: every turn suggested a glimpse of someone slipping out of sight.

We passed slowly among obelisks and angels. The masquerade added a curious potency to our progress. Laura held me tightly, she stroked my hair and I buried my face in her shoulder. She was laughing very softly, right down in her chest, which I could hear because my head was pressed so close. Her heart beat slightly fast, and the sense of it pumping round all this warmth that surrounded me put a choke in my throat and an urgency in my grasp from which Laura wordlessly disengaged herself, pulling me to one side of the path where the leaves partially covered us.

She seemed to swallow before she spoke.

– Two kinds of people haunt cemeteries, she said. Her tone was light and dry but her eyes were anxious. – Ghouls and lovers. Which are you?

It was as if I was a stranger. Her eyes seemed to search my face over and over rapidly but reach no conclusion.

– A widow, I replied, falling in with her formal banter, and touched her hand.

– Why then you're both, she said in a tone at once grave and playful. She turned my hand palm upward and seemed to study if for a moment, then stared at me, slightly embarrassed. I kept my eyes steady and did not betray the strange focus of emotion within me. Then she looked aside, abruptly, and gave a sort of half-smile to distract us both.

– What a place for it, she said, almost under her breath.

She made as if to step onto the path but I caught her hand and held her, determined to take the initiative for once.

– Judy, she said, and there was both alarm and annoyance in her tone.

– I love you, I said stubbornly. I could repeat it without looking at her, and did, trying to get some sense into the words so she could see what I was at.

– Not here, Judy, she said.

Her face registered bafflement and panic.

– There are other places, but not here.

I let her bring me out onto the path. Then I looked up and said with great calmness

– I don't respect the dead.

She looked as if she didn't quite understand me.

– You don't respect them, she said as if making it clear for herself. – Perhaps you should.

Hotel

We were in the foyer of a cheap hotel. Laura was talking to the clerk while I stood by the stairs, gazing up at the short twisted pillars of honey-coloured wood that formed the banisters gradually rising from sight. We had been driving all day, and I was stiff and sweaty from being in the car.

Laura came over.

– Third floor, at the front.

– Sea view, I suggested, beginning to climb the stairs.

– If you look far enough over the roofs.

She sounded tired. I felt a twinge of guilt, moulded into protective compassion. I took one of her bags. My own was very light for there was little in it.

At the top of the shaft a smeared pane admitted the late glow of the sun. Our door was painted white. Once inside, I wedged the window open at the top and pulled the curtains across.

Laura was taking off her shoes.

– Are you hungry? I said on a curious impulse.

– No. Are you?

She looked at me straight for the first time in a while. For a moment I hesitated then smiled and shook my head. I got rather a tight smile in exchange.

– I'm going to sleep, she said and curled up under the coverlet.

I slipped through to the bathroom, ran the tub full of water and soaked there for a long while, topping it up when it threatened to cool. No sound came from the adjoining room. To avoid disturbing her I switched off the bathroom light before opening the door. A faint draught moved the top of the curtain, outlined by a whitish glow that seemed unnervingly precise.

It was some time before I realised I wasn't watching it alone. Then I was careful not to betray my knowledge, relishing the bond that common object gave us. So I was still. And then she turned, and looked at me.

– Couldn't sleep?

– Bad dreams.

I went to sit with her. She sighed, moving up in the bed, then rose abruptly and went to stand by the window. I followed her with my eyes, then looked down, conscious of something I could not share.

– It's cold there, Laura. Come back into bed where it's warm.

She shook her head. I resolved to watch her, then realised with a start that I'd been asleep for a while.

It had been raining for hours. The window was open and she was leaning there, deep in thought, with her chin in her hands.

Sister Anne

One

It is a night in early May, with a sense of the spring just losing its hold. The moonrise is spectacular. It hangs low and heavy over the streets. A red mist covers it, imparting something of a threat.

Nightfall in the suburbs conveys a sense of oppression. Outside a parade of shops, on the corner where three streets cross, the traffic lights change from green to red. For a brief space, at this time of night buses predominate over other traffic. Sometimes the signal goes through red to green and back without anything coming in sight.

A bus draws up past the corner, and a woman gets off. She does not pause or glance at her watch. She does not look behind her, or up. She is wearing a white coat that appears slightly too warm for this time of year. Her shoes are sensibly flat. It is hard to guess her age, but she walks lightly and confidently.

She goes to the end of another street of shops, then turns abruptly down a passage that would hardly be noticed if you didn't know it was there. She walks along between the high damp walls that magnify the sound of her footsteps, imprisoning them oddly, giving the effect of an echo chamber. The passage is so narrow that creepers growing over from the gardens at the back of it touch her shoulder. She smells the faint scent of early buddleia, and almost stumbles, as a squeal suddenly erupts from the broken base of the wall ahead of her. For a moment she hesitates. There are no lights for her to see the rat ahead, but she imagines its footfall, too low for her to hear.

The night watchman sees her approach. He nods as she passes the gate and she gives him a little, tight smile that seems to leave the rounded oval of her face unperturbed. Her smooth blonde hair catches the orange glow of the lamp as she steps beneath.

She enters the main door of the hospital and climbs a narrow flight of stairs that doubles monotonously, meanly, to and fro from the too frequent landings. The walls are tiled part way up, but the tiles have been painted over with a paint that has acquired its shininess from age.

She walks along a narrow corridor, hangs her coat up in a little room and makes some final adjustments to her uniform.

– You're late.

The sister goes off in search of her supper. Anne sits down. There seems to be no reason for nervousness but she looks around her uneasily. From her table with the shadowed lamp she has an oblique view of the ward. As she pours herself a glass of water from the sink and sips it, her expression intensifies.

The arrangement of the ward is a microcosm of the hospital. There is the same mechanical division of space; no disorder to interrupt the sight. Anne takes a little tour up the corridor that runs between the rows of beds. She surveys the sleeping isolated units. She stands for a little while by the window, arms folded and head bowed. Lights from the courtyard penetrate through the half-open blind so she gently pulls it shut.

Half an hour has passed and the sister has not come back. Anne hasn't moved again from her table by the door. However, she displays a new alertness. When a patient coughs she seems almost to jump. Then her attention fixes on the obser vation window that looks into the corridor.

When she hears the steps an extraordinary tension takes possession of her. The slight sharp intakes of breath become more difficult. Her hands seem to grow far away from her. She experiences abrupt dislocation, her heart beats faster and energy floods through her wastefully so it becomes an effort to keep still. She opens the door to the figure standing outside. There is the immediate sense of a conspiracy between them. As the figure enters, without a word, the play of their relationship is apparent. Irritation permeates Anne's excitement. The silent figure's face is ruined, tragic; its huge features collapsed into a kind of harmlessness.

– What goes on?

Una replied slowly, in her low voice

– Sister's gone to the other ward.

– She won't be back?

Una shook her head.

– No, no. Not for a long time.

Anne smiled abruptly, turning her head away though Una couldn't see her anyway in the poor light. The gesture reinforced Una's sense of their separateness. She had something on the tip of her tongue but it froze there as she couldn't find the words to say.

When they sit down it is as if an automatic process has taken over. A concentrated silence wraps them; they have established a communication that makes words irrelevant. Anne takes out a deck of cards, strips off the cellophane, and shuffles them quickly into two piles. Una cuts the nearer heap with a deliberation that is without thought. Anne's hands are restless on the table. Suddenly she begins to deal, five cards each, then stops, raising her eyes to Una's which meet them as if it's the moment they've been waiting for.

To a wakeful patient the scene takes on the quality of a nightmare. First the shadowed lamp is dimmed, until the only light in the ward is a faint blue radiance near the door. When the eyes adjust, there are no shadows, just a swimming darkness which seems tangible in the air around. The eyes blink restlessly, but gain no comfort. Distances are distorted; the end of the bed, no longer visible, seems to have crept up to the chin as if the whole body has shrunken; beyond on either side where there were separate islands of space there is nothing. Sounds muffle and merge in the ever increasing audibility of your own heartbeat.

He can hear footsteps, though, moving slowly up the ward with a brief pause at each bed. A slender shape advances out of the dark, he detects her regular breathing as she bends down near his face. He experiences some indefinable alarm that she will find out he is awake, and tries to hush his breathing right down, desperately praying that his pounding heart will not be heard. For a moment the nurse moves away, then she turns back sharply and he has a sudden, helpless picture of her mind as a game of cat and mouse.

– Can't you sleep, Mr McGregor?

There is nothing in her tone to alarm him. He hears it level, sympathetic, as he has many times before. Yet he can only gabble – The lights. Why have you turned out the lights?

He sees the faint movement as she shakes her head, as if smiling, in the dark. Then she reaches up and the swishing noise betrays that she is pulling the curtains round. He sees the shape of Una advance from the other side. As the curtains meet everything becomes invisible. He is not sure if he has shut his eyes. His mind is blank. He feels the hand stroke his wrist.

– Feeling better?

At the moment he opens his mouth the pillow comes down on his face. He bites feathers through cotton; their prickly mass chokes his throat as the breathing reflex carries on desperately. He does not feel his body arch in its moment of tremendous strength. The nurses hold the pillow in place. Then he is quiet. Anne stands back. She rubs her hand across her mouth; a reaction she cannot analyse. Then suddenly galvanised, she smoothes the old man's night clothes and replaces the pillow behind his head. She slides through the curtains and sets off down the ward at a walk which is not quite a run.

Dr Luther is a young man, always preoccupied. Anne leads him up to the body; he rubs the sleep from his eyes and tries to suppress a yawn in the presence of death. She thinks he has become like a sleepwalker. He nods, then as he becomes aware she sees a slight horror flit across his face.

– I shouldn't have disturbed you, doctor.

Her hand rests on his arm. She removes it lightly.

– Were you here alone?

– Sister's over in the other ward.

He turns automatically to follow the line of her nod. Anne steps back as he examines the man. Una stands at the far side of the bed. Her face is solemn, Anne notes with a sense of irritation, almost pious.

– Just his heart, said the doctor, straightening up.

– Everyone's heart fails in the end, said Anne. – Just a failure to go on living.

She stumbled over the repetition with instinctive calculation. As Dr Luther stared at her, by something in his eyes she could tell she'd shocked him.

– Nurse.

His voice was harsh, after a pause.

When they have watched the porters take the body away Anne stands silent in the little room where they change their clothes. Una watches intently, her face overcast with a strange, innocent terror. Anne's hands hang loose, deliberately non-communicative.

– It's a month.

A vicious sigh indicated her impatience.

– That's average.

– He didn't have much longer to live. To take a week of someone's life isn't much.

The words came after a considerable pause. Anne let her gaze travel along the rows of hooks with names like a school cloakroom.

Una caught her train of thought. It was a familiar one she had long been dreading.

– I don't want to involve someone else.

– I do.

Anne turned back to her. – I'm fed up with going on like this.

Una's face didn't change. Anne controlled her brief outburst, veering away to stare thoughtfully at the names.

– You've been thinking about it for a while, said Una tonelessly.

– You're always the same, said Anne. – Look at you. You're frightened.

She jeered at Una, lifting her hands in the air.

Una looked round, then swiftly grabbed her. They struggled in the middle of the room, swaying round and round against the coats which cushioned the noise of their fight. It was a strange silent dance. The electric bulb was set swinging, sending gigantic shadows over their heads into the corners. At last Una just let go, and they went to opposite sides of the room. Una's breath came in sobs. Anne didn't look at her. She covered her ears with her hands, pushing her head from side to side as if to clear it of some pain or noise.

– Don't touch me again.

– I don't want to get found out, said Una flatly.

Anne looked at her with kindling resentment.

– You never used to mind doing what you were told.

Una's resistance was already weakening. – You treat me so badly, she mumbled rather feebly.

Anne was conscious of letting that go. Then she attacked again.

– Found out. You're stupid. That's the sort of thing I expect from you.

She turned her full gaze on Una, who, after a pause, mumbled uncomfortably. – If you go ahead and ask her, you'll regret it. She's not right. She's too young.

Anne spoke very clearly, with her lips set.

– Who do you think I have in mind?

– Helen, said Una abruptly. Anne's eyes glinted as slits. – If you want her in you can't treat me in this way.

Anne resisted the impulse to bully. Her face became profoundly thoughtful, considering this information. Una waited. At last Anne said

– I'm not supposed to be here.

Una responded with a smile to this peculiarly ingratiating tone. Silently they gathered up their coats, and went separate ways.

Two

Dr Luther was in the arms of his dead wife. His dream was a strange tumble of images that undercut all the feelings he'd ever had about her.

He awoke, sweating, in a panic, with a low moan that left

95

him with a feeling of shame though there was no one to hear. As he switched on the lamp he blinked unsteadily, for a moment thinking, testing, as he tried to clear the persistent dream images from his head.

– Rachel.

Her name seemed to live in the room. He screwed up his hand over his eyes, shaking his head.

In the kitchen, he sipped a glass of milk, and waited for the dream to pass away. Reluctant to go back to bed, he sat down and lit a cigarette.

It was the first night for more than a week that he had been at home. When he put the glass down, his hand trembled, spilling drops of milk. He smoked another cigarette. Five stubs lay in the tray when he next noticed.

Now he knew that he hadn't wanted to come back. He was unable to make peace with what in a moment of self-mockery he called her ghost. If he could just have remembered that he loved her; but so much else was mixed with it. He shivered, remembering the long, cold vigil of her illness when he continually and ineffectually reproached himself with waiting for her to die.

He went slowly to the wardrobe where her clothes were, taking in the faint perfume that still clung. He raked through the dresses, sensing their colours as fragments of a kaleidoscope. Some evoked particular sensations; others – to a sense of guilt evolving within him – not at all. He wondered how he could ever have been unaware of what she wore. At last he opened both doors of the wardrobe, letting the electric light reveal a thin powder of dust over her clothes. He breathed deeply, not from effort, he didn't know why. His hands didn't seem to know what to do – they clenched forgetfully and then hung limp by his sides. He gazed round in the darkness, lowering his head so his shoulders hunched forward a little. There was no analysis possible, just his sense of grief and loss. But how could he grieve, when he doubted that he had loved her? Only by ritual could he overlay his loss with some sense of identity that enabled him to mourn as he thought fit.

He looked to the shelf at the top of the wardrobe. Various

boxes were piled there. He took them down, one by one, mechanically, laid them aside. At the back was a long box that his fingers grasped with difficulty. A slight change came over his face, a look almost of surprise, then his mouth firmed, he took the box and laid it on the bed. It was of a thick, grey, peculiar pasteboard. The lid wasn't taped down so he eased it up with his thumbs. At the corners the wire staples were beginning to rust, leaving their stain about them.

He smelt the camphor, a sharp, clean scent that oppressed his head. He shook it slightly from side to side, seemed to falter for a second, then tossed the mothballs decisively out onto the quilt. Layers of crackling tissue, brittle with age, had to be folded back. He felt the sneeze rising and turned aside.

The white silk caught on his fingers as he raised it from the box. His face was grave, compressed with a sense of inexplicable longing.

He dreamed of their wedding, the church full of white flowers. The figure of the bride beside him, misty pale. The towering wax tapers on the altar, burning with a smooth uninterrupted flame. The bride in her white dress, etherealised from the woman he knew, with the heavy veil covering her face, the veil he couldn't seem to lift. His hands pulled at the white mesh to reveal more material. In a moment, in the vaulted space of the church, he was shrieking and clawing at it, feeling an agonised scream rise from his throat as the figure spun slowly away from him, toppling like a skittle rolling along the floor, to leave yards of white cloth, unravelled like a mummy into an empty heap of clothes.

Three

There is a tall building near the hospital. Strangely isolated among the suburban homes, it looks like a seaside relic, fragile balconies opening onto the side that never gets any sun. There are roughly clipped hedges all around. The paintwork has faded, and is peeling. The five flats on each storey are all rented out. On the top floor, a jet of steam from a pipe indicates that someone is taking a bath.

Over the noise of running water a girl's voice, singing, is barely audible. There is no coherent tune, just a patchwork of fragments running through her head. She breathes out deeply as she gets into the water and watches her feet turn red.

A draught runs through the room which blows the steam every way. Through the open door is another room, filled with the early morning sun. There is an unmade bed, and an empty cot. The baby is asleep in the bed.

Helen turned off the tap and kept humming, splashing the water over herself. In repose, her face had an anxiety that didn't suit it. It had a formless quality that emotion transformed one way or the other.

The baby stirred, coughed, and was quiet. Recalled to him, Helen had a moment of tenderness. Then her face grew set. A bitterness spread over it, refined into lines of passive cruelty. Sometimes she thought all the things that had happened had made her lose her sense of how things are.

She reached up automatically to the shelf for a bottle of red varnish. She had forced herself to do it when she felt her heart was dying. Now she eased her feet up onto the sides of the bath and watched them dry. She smiled to herself as she unscrewed the bottle. The sharp scent made her pull a face. This frivolous ritual was necessary to her precisely because there was no reason for it.

She began grimly enough, but something in the regular action soothed her, and her face absorbed the reflective spell. When she'd finished, she wrapped herself in a towel, and went through.

A desk, neither functional nor decorative, jutted out from one corner of the room. She took a bundle of letters from it, and stood for a moment, indecisive. Then she sat down on the bed and rifled them hastily, leaving the discarded sheets crumpled where her damp hands had moulded the paper. A slight exclamation broke from her, and her face was disturbed with hatred. She brought her hands together in despair, and the expression dissolved until she had a hunted look.

When the baby cried, she picked him up. She felt a strange kind of awe for the intelligence already so separate from her own. In as far as he was an extension of herself she had only a stubborn sense of pity for him.

She reached for the phone and jabbed out a number on the keys. She tapped her fingers as the ringing tone sounded twice, four, six times; then with the expectant start people give when they think their call is answered

– Hello. Is Dr Luther there?

Annoyance grew rapidly on her face as the tape at the other end kept on talking. When the tone came, she waited, then put the receiver down with a loud click.

She left her baby at the crêche and went to work. She was on day shifts, at the hospital.

As she was collecting her things to go home, Anne suddenly appeared in front of her.

– I wanted to see you.

Helen's feelings towards Anne were ambiguous.

– I've got to collect my son.

– I'll come with you, said Anne easily enough. – I came in early on purpose so I could see you.

Helen shrugged. The spell of the day's work was wearing off and she was pleased to have someone to talk to. As they walked together down the corridor she was surprised to find herself relaxing as Anne laughed and joked. She was unusually animated. Helen felt and yielded to the subtle pressures Anne was using to draw her out. She was suspicious and fascinated, sifting each word and reaction for some clue to this sudden interest.

They collected the baby and strolled into the nearby park. For a little while Helen pushed the pram, and Anne, who had fallen silent, wandered beside her. Occasionally she reached out to pluck a sprig from the hedge, sniffing then crushing it thoughtfully so her finger and thumb stained green.

Helen felt an impulse to steer the conversation herself.

– I really don't know anything about you. I've worked here more than a year and I don't know much about anyone.

Anne smiled. – Does it bother you? Her voice sounded very soft. Helen was embarrassed.

– It was a silly thing to say.

She pushed the pram on for a while in silence.

– I know what you mean, said Anne dreamily. She retained the last sprig between her fingers and brought a leaf up to her face. – You can't know what someone's thinking. Or work out the pattern of their life.

Helen lifted her hands from the handle of the pram. – You can see the pattern of my life here.

Anne looked at her, then walked on a few paces before answering.

– That's just superficial.

Her head was turned away so Helen barely heard. She pushed the pram a little faster to catch up.

– You wouldn't like me if I talked about myself, said Anne.

There was a bench just there, sheltered on three sides by a clipped hedge. Helen wasn't sure how they came to be sitting on it. Anne was silent for a few more moments, while Helen rocked the pram with her foot.

– I have no sense of life, said Anne suddenly. – I work, eat, sleep, that's all.

Helen felt she was being fooled.

– Don't go, said Anne when she made to get up.

– I must. I should get him home. I can't think why we're talking like this.

Helen's voice was abrupt but she lingered.

– I wanted to ask you something.

Helen was uneasily intrigued. – Ask me?

– It's not to do with superficial things, Anne said gently. – You must promise not to tell.

She felt the sharpness of Anne's eyes, bidding her, and nodded reluctantly.

– I promise.

– Good, said Anne. There was a little pause as if she was considering something delicate.

– I know your secret.

The words came out so quietly Helen thought she had misheard.

Anne went on without looking at her. – I know you wanted Rachel Luther to die.

Helen put her fist up to her mouth, biting the knuckles till white, shaking her head. In her great success Anne felt a tiny flicker of remorse. She got up and left before Helen recovered her speech.

Four

The shopping precinct led off the main street. It was tiled grey and white. Breathing the recycled air produced a headache.

Dr Luther strolled back to the car park past the empty shops. He was carrying three bags of groceries. As he walked, he hummed. His mind was pleasantly blank. The thoughts that crossed it were all of what he would have for supper.

As he neared the group of ornamental trees, a figure stood up. So far was he immediately absorbed that he didn't stir until she spoke to him.

Her face was vividly drawn as if she hadn't slept. She was dressed very drably with a scarf tied over her head.

He felt as if the ground had been cut from under him. Sensations of shock, regret and guilt blended in an inexpressible confusion. As he struggled to regain his concentration the long-repressed crisis broke.

– I love you.

They made no move towards each other. She looked as if she'd seen something horrible. He stepped back so his right hand came into contact with one of the trees. As he looked at it his face furrowed with disbelief.

– I love you.

She turned abruptly. He said

– What a place!

She laughed as if she was being strangled. He momentarily resented the ugly sound.

– Let's go somewhere else.

His voice had changed.

– What is there for us to say to each other, she replied. – Rachel is dead. We can't do anything about it now.

He felt horror in his turn.

– You talk as if I killed her.

101

Helen turned back to him. – You feel that we killed her. You feel revulsion for those nights we arranged while someone else looked after her. Your guilt puts itself on me.

She spread her hands wide. He stared vaguely at the space of air they measured.

– It's no one's fault. It couldn't be helped.

– That's no excuse now, she said brokenly. – It's all gone wrong.

She shook her head, not looking at him.

He couldn't ask her why she was like this, or comfort her. He felt a terrible dislocation himself, as if her despair had poisoned him. He had a visual image of her face choking, drowning. He couldn't trust himself, he was incapable of acting or wanting any more.

He pushed past her out into the car park. The cloying fumes of petrol hit him.

– Why struggle, why resist, he thought wildly. – It's how I am. Every time it traps me.

He got into his car and just sat there, with the sense of something terrible pressing him down. He let his head fall forward on the steering wheel and his lips moved, making a chorus of the two women's names.

Five

Una turned to Anne slowly.

– I didn't want you to get her in.

– I know.

Anne cut across Una's protest, then stopped as if the words had run out.

– What did she say? Una persisted.

Anne's face seemed puffy and tight.

– I didn't ask her.

Una's face registered blankly, then she put her hand up to her mouth to hide her delight.

– Don't, said Anne roughly. – Don't crow over me.

Una had never seen her so confused, reflective.

– It seemed too ridiculous when I started, said Anne

102

slowly. – Why should she have believed me.

– What did you do?

Anne snapped suddenly back into herself.

– Never mind.

Una was brave. – You failed, she said suddenly.

– Animal! Anne snapped out. – I could do anything, anything I want, she repeated slowly.

She walked up and down a little to regain her composure. Then some idea seemed to take possession of her features.

– Una, she began dreamily. – What would you do if we were found out?

– What are you thinking of? said Una. Anne smiled at the fear in her voice.

– It wouldn't make any difference to me.

Una bit her lip, struggling to control her resentment and answer calmly.

Anne smiled.

– How many people do you think have been like us?

She sat down quietly and put her head in her hands.

– Who knows the acts we commit in our dreams?

– Stop it, said Una roughly, with a sense of panic that she was being mocked. Anne's face was raised to her with an expression of wonder, then she began to laugh. There was a note of distress in it that disturbed Una.

– Perhaps we shouldn't do it any more, she said very quietly. – Perhaps we've both had enough. Your wanting to bring in Helen showed that it had changed. It's not like it used to be.

She could tell from the reaction that this wasn't what Anne had expected. Her face changed. There was the expression of confusion again, then she nodded.

– I don't think I've ever heard you say so much.

There was a return to the old tone, but she smiled and her face cleared as she felt a sense of liberation. She stood up. There was intense uncertainty in her face, as if she was struggling to pierce the idea of her own identity.

– See you, said Anne abruptly, and left the room.

Una waited for her to come back, growing increasingly

uneasy. The sudden dissolution of their compact left her with a sense of loss mingled with fear that now Anne might go to the police. She dismissed this as unreasonable but the idea kept recurring. She thought of herself painted by Anne as a villain, a monster.

– I'm not, she repeated under her breath. – I'm not.

She had a feeling of outraged innocence. She said to herself – I couldn't help it.

This was no comfort. The fear of possible betrayal would not go away.

Six

The heat of the afternoon blazed into the ground.

Helen was sitting alone in the park. Her eyes were closed and on her face was a stunned look. All around people were stretched in various attitudes on the borderline between consciousness and sleep. The sun shone through her lids, giving the impression of looking into a glowing darkness.

She heard a footfall hesitate near her but didn't want to look. She waited for it to pass on. Dr Luther stood gazing down at her. He had been studying the faces of all the sleepers. His expression was strangely nostalgic.

– Helen.

With reluctance she opened her eyes. There was no surprise in her face. Then she smiled, expressing a multitude of feelings. She gazed at him, resigned to her incomprehension.

– Let's get married.

– What, be your second wife? she murmured as if this had disturbed her. She raised herself on one elbow and looked at him intently. He felt a stirring of impatience, but bore the scrutiny. At last she said

– When?

He was nettled by her casualness.

– Whenever you like.

He took one of her hands and she did not resist. Then she started to laugh.

– What's so funny?

– I don't know. After all this time, it just seems so strange.

They kissed, feeling a physical sympathy which was at the same time oddly alienating. Then she frowned slightly, speaking with a note of genuine regret.

– I have to go to work.

– So have I, he said with a feeling close to shame.

From where she stood Anne watched them cross the park and pass through the hospital gates. Her face was an unguarded picture of dissatisfaction.

She struck her fists together lightly and turned away from the window. Her expression betrayed that she was going over something rapidly but purposelessly in her head.

Una came into the room. Anne looked embarrassed, she bewildered. At length their eyes met.

– Are you getting along all right?

Una paused, then nodded.

– I got myself transferred to day shifts, too.

– That's nice.

Anne spoke non-committally, avoiding the meaning implicit in Una's tone.

Una's face cleared a little.

– I came to find you so we could give Mrs Travis her bath.

– But I've just finished, said Anne. – Get Helen to help you. She just came in.

– Sister said you were to help me.

– She did not.

They stared at each other. Eventually Anne said

– Is this a threat?

Una shook her head.

– No. Self-preservation.

Anne stirred.

– You always despised me, said Una. – I could go and tell Sister right now. You always said you didn't care about being found out. Here's your chance to prove it.

– You wouldn't do it, said Anne. – You value your own safety too much.

Irritated, she turned back to the window with a dismissive gesture.

– But it is my safety, Una said. – Otherwise I'll always be worrying.

Her voice dropped. Anne turned back to her. Her face was thoughtful but curiously absent.

– You should have trusted me.

– Why?

– Because I like secrets, Anne said quietly.

Una stared at her. She felt a delicate recognition, anticipatory of regret.

– Let's give Mrs Travis her bath.

– No!

– But you wanted to, said Anne in the same quiet tone.

– I don't know now.

Anne smiled faintly. – I'll go home then.

Something in her tone asserted the authority she had regained.

– No, wait! Una cried as she turned to go.

Anne spoke with her back to her. She repeated

– It's your choice, Una.

– Yes.

The word was barely audible. Anne turned round. There was a slight wildness in her eyes that struck Una as unfamiliar.

They walked down the corridor. Una kept glancing nervously at her companion. As they passed the Sister she looked at them a little surprised.

They entered the geriatric ward. Mrs Travis was in the second bed on the left. Una stiffened slightly, almost reluctant to approach, but Anne touched her arm casually with fingers that felt like steel.

Mrs Travis turned her head from side to side. She smiled at the two nurses standing at the foot of her bed.

– You've come to bathe me.

Una nodded. Anne went to the top of the bed. For some reason she took the old woman's hands and stroked them.

– You look fine today Mrs Travis.

– Thank you, dear.

She looked up into their faces, then said

– You mustn't mind if I cry out at first. The water feels

strange on my skin, but I get used to it quickly.

They put her in a wheelchair and took her to a cubicle. She sat quietly while Una ran the bath and Anne fussed around, cutting her fingernails and toenails. As she combed her hair, Mrs Travis smiled.

– Shall I wash it? said Anne, glimpsing Una's frightened face through the steam.

– It doesn't matter.

The taps were turned off. In the silence Mrs Travis sighed. Anne caught Una's eyes; held them nodding imperceptibly.

– I'm getting cold.

Mrs Travis' voice had lost its spirit. She was hunched forward, glum like a child. They took her by the shoulders and legs to ease her into the water. For the moment she seemed about to fall back Anne pillowed her head with her hands. As she glanced up Una was struck by the hallucinatory quality of her face.

– You're a good nurse, said Mrs Travis with difficulty. – You're...

Anne pushed her head down beneath the water. Una moved automatically, grabbing the legs to hold them still as the feet kicked out repeatedly. The old woman's arms thrashed, soaking their aprons. In less than a minute she was dead.

They both stepped back. Anne's lip was bleeding where she had bitten it. Una's face, flushed with the exertion, was rapidly paling. – I liked her, said Anne quietly.

Their eyes met. As the door opened, they turned to see the Sister and Helen, their faces blank at the scene before them. With a quick glance at the nurses, the Sister padded across the wet floor to raise the corpse's head.

– Has there been an accident here? she said after a stunned pause.

With her finger on her lip to staunch the blood Anne smiled wearily at her disbelief.

– We all did it. We're guilty, aren't we, Una, Helen?

Then she let her chin sink down into her neck.

– It really doesn't mater, she murmured twice. – It doesn't matter at all.

The Girlfriend

One

His eyes were the first thing I noticed about him. Danny and I were eating breakfast at a table in the hotel. This stranger across the way tried ostentatiously not to look at us but I still felt his stare. Dan had his back to him, I was sitting at a slight angle and so caught his view sideways, seemingly absorbed in his coffee and newspaper. And so he was. But in us. Every time I glanced across to Dan I seemed to feel his eyes tighten and renew their hold.

– Someone's looking at us.

– Have some more coffee.

– Who is he?

– You'll have to get used to him.

– Who is he?

– He's my shadow.

I'd come to the hotel the night before. It was in a run-down skiing resort, in summer, the time you'd expect to find no one there. Dan had a good reason for being there, so did I. It was connected with him. The hotel was empty apart from a British couple, and the stranger.

– He follows me around, said Dan, pouring some more coffee. – He's harmless, Nicky. He even comes across and talks to me sometimes.

He smiled at me. – We chat. Not about anything important.

– Why does he follow you?

– You're not stupid, Nicky. Have some more bread, you've hardly eaten anything. We have a long walk ahead of us through the Alpine scenery.

With that, he turned and smiled at his shadow, who acknowledged him with a faint movement of his eyes.

– Do you want to come with us?

– I've got some business around town this morning, said

the shadow, getting up.

– Your work is never done.

I could tell Dan was slightly rattled, that in spite of pretending otherwise this figure got to him.

– Let me introduce you to Nicky. She's my girlfriend.

I glanced up quickly and smiled.

– Pleased to meet you.

– Have a good morning, Tom.

Dan spoke his name at the last minute with a sort of jeer. The stranger lifted his hand. After he'd left the room Dan went across to his table and picked up the paper he'd left behind. He came back slowly and sat down, rustling the pages.

– Don't you want to talk to me?

He ignored me but he didn't appear to be reading it. Instead he was searching all along the columns, running his finger down the blank spaces of each page.

– He's done a picture of you!

– Let me see.

Dan hung over it for a minute, then passed it across.

– Not much of an artist, I remarked.

– I don't know.

He suddenly seemed in better spirits. – Old Tom must have hidden depths, he said, laying his hand lightly on my shoulder. – Or perhaps he was just memorising your features so if ever he comes across you on your own you can lead him to me.

I followed him up the stairs to our room. He sat down on my bed nearest the window with his binoculars.

– So old Tom has gone to the bank to draw out his expenses.

– He's here to catch you.

I sat down beside him.

– He won't catch me.

– Why are you worried then?

He didn't reply, but got up and paced around.

– I was just thinking, Nicky.

I lay back on the bed with its ridiculously snowy pillows.

– Has he got anything against you?

– There is nothing against me.

He recrossed the room to the window and leant on the sill. I reached up from where I was lying and put my hands on his shoulders.

– Shall I make you better, Dan?

He moved his shoulderblades under my touch. I massaged him slowly, then suddenly he broke away.

– What an angel you are, Nicky.

– Irony's wasted on the infatuated.

He turned around, then smiled at me.

– You do a good job, Nicky. I'll say that for you.

– What more could you expect?

He took my hand a moment, then dropped it.

– I've never pretended that I loved you.

– No.

– You mustn't make yourself bitter, Nicky. You know no one can do that to you but yourself.

– Why's that man after you? I said, wanting violently yet half-heartedly to wound that sanctimonious tone.

– I told you he's my shadow. It's his job to follow me around. Like the moon follows the sun; except that perhaps you're my moon, Nicky, sweet and sad, feminine, patient, in the shadows.

There was a profound silence during which I bit my lip. He sensed something of this, and even relented a minute.

– You'd never believe that I don't mean to be cruel to you.

– Make me more of a fool than I already am.

– You're a free agent, Nicky.

– I repeat that to myself at nights.

He laughed, then walked round the room restlessly. – Let's go down into the garden.

As we walked round the paved yard dotted with bright geraniums, I was aware of the stranger sitting on the terrace.

– Why don't you go and talk to him, Nicky?

– Is it important to you? I said roughly.

He looked at me, then shook his head decisively. – No. I just want to see what you make of him. And what he makes of you.

His eyes glinted. I shook his hand off my arm.

– He likes you.

– How can you tell?

He didn't react to the disgust in my voice. Instead he laughed and led me away.

– When someone's been following you for a while you get to know them pretty well. Observation is a two-way process. When you watch someone, you lay yourself open to being watched. I've made him hate his job. He feels he's been drawn into a disgusting intimacy. I've made sure he knows everything about me. Even when I clean my teeth sometimes I'll stand at the window if I know he's there so he'll have to watch me. He just can't turn away from me. If I hid, resented his presence, his job would be a lot easier. And Nicky...

Suddenly he kissed me. We were still in full view of the terrace. I struggled back, and slapped his face. There was a stinging red mark across his cheek but he smiled, not resenting it.

– ... That'll be something interesting for him to work on. Perhaps the next time you help me in my play-acting you'll have the grace to pretend that you enjoy it.

Two

We left the resort, travelled down by the Italian lakes in some strange parody of an eighteenth-century Grand Tour. We went by train, stopping off in small villages where Dan would disappear for hours and I would lie quietly in the sun or stir myself to look round in a touristy way. It was what was expected of me. I was an actress playing a part and I did it automatically: it had got into my very flesh, so that I was no longer conscious of it. I was his alibi, his witness. In a strange way I felt I had appointed myself his guard. I lost myself in musty old churches where paintings must have glowed deep colours once but were now faded with age. I hung around city squares in open-toed sandals, fed pigeons, studied guidebooks, and mingled with the crowd. But I never spoke to any of them; the semblance was enough. Any real relationship,

111

even casual acquaintances, posed a threat to Dan and through him, to myself. There is a kind of remoteness you can attain. As we travelled south I acted older, and we worked together to project the image of a honeymoon couple. Although we were apart most of the days, there were moments in suitably romantic trysts which would find us locked in a passionate embrace. The passion was on my side, the acting all on his. Yet I was never sure to what degree he faked it. Sometimes I almost believed he returned my feelings or had made himself think so. It was bitter and irresistible. When we walked together along the shore of a lake, the people who passed us left us alone with no more than a sly glance under their lashes, followed by the benign smile bestowed upon lovers.

The watcher was still with us, though he seemed to leave us alone a great part of the time. Dan laughed at this, said he'd managed to drive him away. He added that sometimes when he was alone he'd noticed Tom following him, seen his figure step quickly aside into a building or behind a tree as he passed.

– He tried to frighten me at first, but now he sees it isn't any good.

He was at the window of our room again, kneeling on the seat to peer out through his binoculars. It happened several times a day. Dan chuckled.

– He's gone shy. He's squeamish.

He turned. – Got you to thank for that.

I stretched carefully, lazily on the honeymooners' bed. Spending all this time with him I was learning a little to hide my feelings.

– I'm glad I'm so useful to you.

– You're useful all right.

He got up and came over to me, smiling.

– I still wish you'd talk to him.

– Tell him all your secrets?

– No.

He sat down beside me, ran his hand along my arm.

– You'd never betray me.

– Why not.

He smiled.

– It's not in your nature.

I studied him. – No, I wouldn't, I said softly at last.

He got up again, smiling more uneasily. I could see, day by day, how he was growing a little more rattled. Although he boasted that Tom was failing to keep up his surveillance, I had some idea that he'd preferred it when he was constantly aware that he was followed, and at least knew where Tom was. The idea of him being unaccounted for made him nervous. He couldn't be sure when he was and was not watched, or what else Tom might be up to.

I could have told him, but it was part of the slight hardening in me that I didn't. It gave me a little piece of self-respect, this independence, as well as a more nebulous feeling that this was some slight retaliation for the wear he subjected me to from day to day.

When I went out in the mornings to the café across the square, I would sit at a corner table, order fruit juice and coffee, and a bread roll. I would deliberately crack the roll in half and butter it with the feeling of a sacramental act. I would sip half the fruit juice very slowly, and nibble the roll, and by the time I got to a certain bite and a certain level down the glass, Tom would always appear. He sat two tables across from me with his paper, and would drink and read, but I was always aware of the intensity of those eyes upon me. To speak to each other was taboo, but I felt I knew him. He was the secure point in my life; living with Danny was a constant set of emotional shifts. The nearest we came to communication was one day when he got up rather suddenly before I'd finished and walked out, brushing against my table as if accidentally on his way to the door so the newspaper was dislodged. I gathered it up unsteadily, my heart already beating much too fast as I slowly unfolded the crumpled pages. On the inside of the fold was written in large capitals with a blunt pencil.

'VOUS SOUFFREZ – QUITTEZ LUI – IL VOUS FAIT MAL'   .

Written in French to misdirect attention. It occurred to me that he couldn't speak Italian. No wonder he'd dropped out of sight so much. I laughed, mirthlessly, and left the paper lying on the table.

Most of the furnishings in the hotel were red plush, highly-polished mahogany and good old mirrors. It was the most expensive hotel in the town. I knew Danny was handling a lot of money but still I suspected his main reason for staying there was that Tom would not be able to afford it. The dining-room looked over the lake. There were tall, old windows, still holding the original glass which hadn't been replaced with plate. The heavy, red curtains hung in dignified, carefully dusted knots, as I ran my fingers up against the pile. Doing so made me wince but I couldn't resist it. I stared at the rain spattering the glass to blur the grey view of the lake. Dinner would be ready in a few minutes. I was wearing a black dress with a strange hooped overskirt of net, which I disliked. It was suitably stuffy for the grand hotel, Danny had said when he chose it.

The shape of a man came up behind me; I saw the reflection in the blurred glass. I didn't bother to turn at first, struggling with my resentment at Danny; I would have to look at him soon enough. Then something in the posture, the very way he remained still behind me, made me turn.

He looked as ill at ease in his borrowed suit as I felt in that dress. We stared at each other, then his eyes intensified.

– I must talk to you. Only for a moment.

I fumbled with the latch on the French window, then we stepped out onto a balcony. It was only a few feet above the ground but the wind and rain drove with considerable force. I stepped back against the wall where there was a little shelter.

– You must go.

I hadn't spoken a word, only looked at him. His expression changed again. He said slowly

– I can't do anything while you're here.

– That's why I'm here, I said simply.

He seemed taken aback.

– You're wasting your time.

I smiled, and turned to go back in.

In the light of the chandeliers the raindrops caught on my skirt were like diamonds. I walked across to the long table where the guests and visitors dined. Danny was making his way across, smiling at me fondly. The waiters were already drawing the curtains across the rapidly darkening view.

The table glittered with lights. Dan drew out my chair and sat down next to me. There was the gleam of candles on fine old silver and the ridiculously plump white napkins. Danny was beginning to enjoy himself as he rarely did. Something of the routine, the very elegant stuffiness of the dinner appealed to him. As I reached forward to unroll my own napkin, he was doing the same, then I was suddenly jolted to realise that his hands were frozen in mid-air. I heard him say

– Hullo, Tom, in a voice that sounded normal but had a tremor behind it. Then he put the napkin down and said quietly – Are you playing the ghost at the feast?

Tom said – Macbeth, and Lady Macbeth too, with a glance in my direction. Then he smiled.

– I've come to see how the rich live.

– We're flourishing. As you can see.

– In this hole. In these barracks...

Tom was perceptibly angry. As if at a loss for what to say he turned to me again.

– Quite a different picture from the schoolgirl I saw first.

– This is more accurate, I said faintly, forcing myself to meet his eyes. But he wouldn't look at me. Danny picked up on this, but said nothing. He started to eat his dinner when it arrived. Neither Tom nor I touched ours, though Danny kept urging me after every second mouthful.

When the next course came, I excused myself and left. Neither of them followed. As I looked back from the shadow of the revolving door I saw them staring at each other across the table.

Three

When Danny got back he wouldn't say a word. I had seen him in such moods before, but never this bad. He was terrifying, but I knew just to lie on the bed and ignore him. I watched covertly as he moved round the room, gathering and rejecting

115

his belongings until he had only enough for a small case. I waited until it was completely packed before I said, slowly

– Where are you going?

As he stood and looked at me his eyes glittered.

– Away.

– Shall I stay here?

He took a wad of money from his pocket and deposited it on the table.

– What about Tom?

– Keep him here if you can.

– Why should I be able to do that? I muttered.

Not replying, he busied himself tidying a few things. As I watched him I despised myself.

– Don't leave me, Danny.

He passed in front of the mirror so I saw his face. His eyes met mine in the reflection, but he was staring at himself. At last he said

– I must go, Nicky.

He came over and kissed me, but it was the one time that I was cold to him. I simply turned my face away. He released me and stood there, looking down at me.

– Buying my loyalty.

– Look, Nicky, when this is all over we'll go away somewhere together and have a real holiday.

I got up and went over to the window. – It'll never be over.

I heard the door click as he slipped out, but forced myself to stare at the rain for a few seconds longer. Only when I heard the far-off bang of an outside door did I pull the curtains across abruptly and turn back into the room. I had a humiliating picture of myself running out after him into the rain. I made myself lock the door and undressed, lying down on the huge bed where we had slept night after night without touching. I moved across to the side where he'd have been. I couldn't help it. In the dark the room still retained something of his presence. I was in agonising pain. Now, by myself, I didn't feel that I could function. While he was there my life had revolved round him, now his absence was all that occupied me.

The next morning I asked to be moved to a smaller room on a different floor. I put Danny's stuff out of sight, but still everything in the room contrived to remind me of him.

I went out to the café on the square, well after my usual time. Tom wasn't there. I ate my breakfast slowly, drank two more cups of coffee, but he didn't show. Somehow this completed my desolation. It meant that he had followed Danny after all. I felt I ought to be relieved but I missed him. Having got used to the sense of being watched I felt strangely isolated. At last I left the café and strolled round the village. His surveillance had given some meaning to my pointless walks; without him I felt like a boat cut loose, some wretched bit of cork bobbing about, doing nothing on the open sea.

I wanted to buy some cigarettes. I was just going up the steps of the shop when the door opened and Tom came out. We were face to face for a moment. He registered shock. I moved back automatically onto the pavement. As we lingered there it struck me that there was no longer any reason for us not to speak.

– You know he's gone?
– I suggested it last night.
We were walking along the pavement together.
– But you stay here?
– He'll come back.
– You're very sure.
He stopped.
– Then I stick with you.
– Do you think he'll come back to me?
I wasn't sure he could read my smile, but he appeared to. He nodded very slightly.
– I wish I was that certain, I said, walking on.
– You love him.
– I don't know.
He stopped again, putting his hand on my arm and looked straight at me. I glanced at him then, with a sort of shame, as I remembered Danny's injunction to keep him there, shook myself free.

He didn't follow me. After that, he kept out of sight.

There was a boat which took trips up and down the lake. It was cool, and usually not too busy. I had Danny's money to waste and made the trip almost every afternoon. The breeze was pleasant, and even the smell of the lake had a strange sort of appeal. Out of habit, as I got on, I looked round at my fellow passengers, but was met with blank stares. The engine of the boat was started and we chugged towards the distant mountains. I stood in the bows and peered over at the white wake of the boat, churning the water in a choppy, oil-smelling trail. As the town receded behind us, my heart lifted. Every afternoon at least, this limited escape was allowed me. Suddenly the overcast sky seemed to clear a little and the sun emerged; I glanced up and caught the quick bright flash of something reflective being lowered hastily.

There was a hut some way up the mountain from that point on the shore. It had been a shepherd's hut, but was now empty, the captain of the boat informed me. I smiled uncertainly, my head full of crazy plans. Back at the hotel, I ate some fruit, then waiting till almost dusk, set off along the path by the shore. The noises of the town behind me gradually faded, giving way to the rural sounds of the landscape and waves washing gently against the pebbles. Sometimes I whistled to keep myself from thinking, sometimes stopping uncertainly as some particular call through the night gave me a sensation of alarm. The darkness was warm, dark blue. There were few stars overhead. Nearing the hut, I went more slowly as there came a final uncertainty about what I would find.

I climbed the slope. There were scrubby pine trees all bent over with their roots arched above the ground where it had fallen away. I avoided the path, because the small stones would warn whoever was in the hut of my approach, and inched my way up on fingers and toes over the pine needles, releasing their sharp dry scent and pricking my hands. When I reached the hut, I stood quietly listening for any sounds inside. If there was someone, they must be asleep. I walked cautiously round, but there were no windows. Still, I felt that my presence had disturbed the occupant. The silence seemed more intense, as if a waiting game had developed there, in the empty night. The units of time did not slip past, but were measured. I stood outside the door feeling my heart was in my mouth, then very gently I raised the latch. With the sensation of walking into a trap I pushed the door open and stepped inside.

Nothing happened. I struck a match. Temporarily blinded by the flash, at last I saw Tom lying under a heap of sacks in a corner of the hut looking up at me. The match went out underfoot. I shut the door. He said

– Who were you expecting to find, Nicky?

– Were you expecting me? I said softly.

He didn't answer.

– So you let the sun catch your binoculars on purpose this afternoon?

– You might have known that and still come up.

– Why do you think I came?

– I don't know, he said evasively after a long silence.

– Tom, I said. – Why are you here? What good does it do you to follow us around?

– You wouldn't understand.

There was another pause. – You love him.

– If I said I loved you?

– Then I'd say he put you up to it.

– You don't think I have any will of my own?

He sighed.

– I think love can distort your will. It can spoil your sense of who you are and why you do things. Do you think I'm doing my job here, having let him go?

There was silence. I couldn't reply. He spoke my name quietly. As I walked over, my shoes clinked against something metallic on the floor. His hand reached it quickly before I could, tossed it away.

– Self-protection. – What from? What's the point?

I lay down beside him, and he tentatively moved on top of me. I lay tense, appalled at the mixture of my feelings, aware of the uncomfortable sacking beneath me, staring into the darkness past his head. Then he rolled aside and I could hear him breathing very fast.

– I can't do this, Nicky.

His voice was more of a groan. – Not with you lying here thinking every minute of him. I thought I could. I love you. I wish you'd come with me or go anywhere away from him.

I was silent.

– He said you wanted to save me.

– Save you?

He laughed bitterly. – I can't save myself. I made an agreement with him which I knew he'd break.

– What did you agree?

He was silent.

– That you'd drop everything against him if he never saw me again?

Will you keep to it?

– What else can I do?

There was silence. Then I said

– There's something else.

– How do you mean?

– Well there is, isn't there?

He sighed.

– I didn't want you to hate me, Nicky. I stole his letter to you. It arrived at the hotel this morning, telling you that he was coming back tonight.

– Then you lured me up here? So Danny's at the hotel now, waiting for me?

He nodded. I started to laugh.

– I think it's the best thing I ever heard.

Spike and Scissors

I have spent the whole morning trying to write it, but can never find the right words. Yesterday I went and walked about the streets, looking at advertisements, staring at the headlines on boards outside shut newsagents. The people who write them must have such a gift – for a snappy way of putting things, a way of arranging words so it grabs your attention and strikes you as just right. I suppose it's mainly practice, but however many times I try, I always seem to get stuck. Just a few words in, and already I'm making mistakes. I once read a book where there was a character who could never get past the first sentence of the novel he was writing. Well I have no such ambitions. I never read novels – not now. But I'm digressing – that's one thing I learnt from novels, anyhow, that you can ramble on and on, till you wind it up, ever so neatly, back at the beginning. So you don't have to cross anything out. That's good, I hate crossing out – that's why I'm writing a diary. No one will ever read it, so I don't have to bother. Perhaps I'd better say what I was trying to write – my diary doesn't know yet, because it was all quite clean and blank ten minutes ago, and had less idea about me than the pavement outside. After all, I walk on that pavement every day, stepping on the same lines if I remember. But my diary is learning about me quite rapidly. There is growing satisfaction in turning the pages, watching my handwriting run over the clean paper, till the black marks fill a double spread and when I turn the page, I can see the shadow of my words clearly indented. I have never written so much before, and the excitement is unbearable.

It is nearly twelve o'clock. I put down my pen, rummage beside the cooker for two carrier bags, and go out to do my shopping at the supermarket. I go there every day at exactly the same time.

There were a few things I needed – butter, milk, eggs, two tins of fish, some bread – a forced compromise – and shampoo.

I feel quite bad about the bread. I've tried ever so many ways of getting round the problem, but there seems to be nothing that I can eat which isn't made from plants. Sometimes I go quite red, thinking about it, and can only reassure myself by arguing that, after all, the wheat has gone through so many extreme processes on its way to being a loaf that it's extremely unlikely to be hurt by what I do to it. But that isn't a very satisfying theory. So I wrap up the loaf, when I get home, in two plastic bags, and hide it under the sink where there's a cupboard which is very cold and dark. There are lots of plants in the room – I hope they're not too offended by its presence.

When I've selected my food, I pick up another wire basket and head for the vegetable counter.

There is nothing much here today. An old woman next to me is picking up the potatoes one by one, weighing them in her hands, picking out the largest. The assistant gets impatient, and suggests she weigh them. The old woman snarls at her and starts to abuse the produce. I keep out of it, and walk briskly towards the green stuff.

Lettuces and cabbage. It hurts me to see them like this, in the tight plastic bags with the leaves all bruised and wrinkling under electric light. I pick them up, one by one, to look at the cut stalks, where the sap just dried. Only the youngest and freshest are worth getting. The assistant sighs irritatingly, and I look at her to get her to shut up. Then she loses interest. A middle-aged man with two children demands all her attention. They have seen the chocolate-coated apples, and are furiously trying to reach them. Their father tells them not to as one knocks down a cascade of lemons onto the floor. Most roll away unharmed, but one is squashed by a trolley. The pips explode across the polished surface. I choose my lettuce and turn my back on the horrid sight. One of the children is crying, and I notice the potato woman in front of me. Her bag bulges, but the wire basket is empty. She wanders out, looking unconcerned. From my place in the queue at the cash desk, I see her stopped by a store employee, who gestures as if courteously demanding the basket. She drops it on his foot. I lean forward to pay for my goods. The girl at the cash desk gives me a receipt, which I put in the bag with the milk. Then I head out. These automatic doors are a good invention, because I always have two bags, and I can't risk letting them touch each other.

Back home, I switch on the radio and listen to the news in a half-hearted sort of way, not really taking it in, but at least putting off the time when I will have to get down to work again. I don't mind writing this diary, I really don't. It's so much easier than my – what's the word – polemic. I keep wanting to put 'essay' but of course that isn't really right. The more I think about this polemic, the more hopeless I feel. I find writing so difficult. I know what I feel, but when I come to put it down, it seems all wrong. So stiff. And I can't talk about it either. I once tried to, in the street, and people thought I was hysterical. So I thought I would start a diary, and put down what I do, and what I feel when I do it, so that I would get into the habit of feeling more clearly, and could write it down so that people would understand me and take notice. I thought the bit with the lemons was quite good, so perhaps I am becoming more expressive. I must write down everything I do in my diary. That will help me.

There is a knock at the door, which I take some time to answer because I am finishing this sentence. When I open it, it's the landlord. He comes round for a chat sometimes. I give him a glass of water, and say something about writing a cheque. He looks around the room while I am writing this.

He is admiring my big tubs of earth, poking his finger delicately into the soil. I don't think he likes it very much. He sips his glass of water. I am looking up from behind the chest of drawers where I am pretending to rummage for my cheque book. He asks if I am planning to grow trees. I say that I was, but changed my mind. He's not really interested, just slightly puzzled. I don't think he likes the idea of trees much, but few landlords would be as patient about all the other plants, and taking furniture out of the room when there's no more room for it. The chest of drawers and a chair are the only things left. Almost the whole floor is covered with plant pots. When I look at them sometimes it makes me feel proud to think that I carried them home, one by one, all by myself in the space of a year. The fridge is working fine, I say in answer to his query. It's just that I've just been to the shop and it's full of food – that's why the lettuces are on the windowsill. They keep well in water. Yes, it is hot.

He is silent, looking out of the window, and at last I have a chance to write that cheque. Speech looks so odd on the page – what would he think if I told him I had been writing down all that he said, and what I think about it. Another glass of water? No. He has gone.

I sometimes wonder if I'm lonely. I know that I used to have friends, and that we'd go out to the pub together, and sometimes to parties. We'd never really talk to each other, and I don't think they took life very seriously. I liked enjoying myself, but I used to wake up in the middle of the night and ask myself what I was doing. The darkest hour is just before dawn, and all that sort of thing. I would forget about it, and drift back to sleep, and in the morning it would seem like nothing had happened. Of course, there were books I used to read, and some of them would talk about how we had no place on this earth, and that we weren't really real, just shadows in the mind of someone else, and how there was a dark fist of despair just waiting to crush us in its grip. And how life was terrible, and full of pain. Well of course I know that's true now, but at the time I didn't give a shit. I thought these books were funny; I still do, but now for a different reason, that anyone would need it pointing out to them. So I went on going to parties, and at one someone got more than usually drunk and smashed a bottle into their boyfriend's face. I thought I'd done it, though everyone said it was someone else, and how they hadn't really done it on purpose, just slipped because they were so drunk. But the scream he gave when he was hit with the bottle, and the blood running off his face onto the floor, did something to me inside, and I stopped going to parties, and went somewhere I wouldn't have to see those people anymore. It all looks a bit odd when I write it down. I can't remember enough of what happened to make it clear. I knew that I couldn't stand the sight of pain, and yet there was nothing I could do about it. The sound he made when he was hit went right through me – and yet I found, when I was staring at the blood, that the sight did not displease me. It flowed out of his wounds, looking clean and fresh, and somehow I just couldn't stop staring at it. It was so peaceful. There he was, lying unconscious – and the blood, thickening slightly at source, soaking down into the carpet, making a larger stain.

I couldn't cope with my feelings. I had to admit that I liked the sight of blood, even if I couldn't stand the pain that would cause it to flow. Or, to put it the other way round, as I succeeded in doing after several weeks of thought, I hated the causing of pain, but my hatred would be qualified where the pain led to such a strangely pleasurable result.

I considered suicide. What could be better than watching my own blood flow? But the thought of the pain involved dissuaded me. I purchased a knife, and even ran the blade along my skin experimentally. But my head swam, and a few moments later I was being violently sick. How could I manage these feelings? It was like being torn in two. Everywhere I went I would crave the sight of blood, and would stand dizzily outside butchers, fascinated and repelled as a man drew a knife across what had once been living flesh.

And then, quite by chance, I discovered how I could redirect my energies. I was walking through a park, quite late in the afternoon, my head still reeling from my experiences at the shops, when there was a warning shout, and two kids, aged about nine, hurled a stick up into the tree I was walking underneath. I dodged out of the way, and the stick, with a great rustling and rattling, came back to earth, bearing what looked like about half a branch with it. It was a chestnut tree, obviously enough. The children searched the branch eagerly for conkers, stripped off half a dozen unripe pods, and ran off.

125

I had walked on a little way, but came back when I heard them go.

The branch was lying on the ground. A few leaves still clung to it. Not knowing quite why I did so, I stooped to pick it up, and examined the place where the stick had caught it, and torn it from the tree. The branch was old and rotten – the bark crumbled off under my fingers – but when I looked at the end which had been severed, it seemed fresh, and I could trace the pattern of the damaged fibres. They stuck out, clean, white, and slightly twisted by the force of the blow which had brought the branch down.

I craned upwards at the tree and thought I could make out where it had come from, a dim white spot almost hidden by the leaves which were just beginning to turn. I ran my hand along the branch, feeling for each jagged knot where the conkers had been pulled off. In each place, the slightest of wounds. I stared at the branch with a dizzy idea of what this meant. It had never occurred to me before that plants could feel, but at that moment, with the branch clasped firmly between my hands, I experienced a sickening surge of pain in sympathy with the tree. It lasted a second, and when it was gone I drew a deep breath and looked at the branch between my hands with fresh respect. The twisted fibres were still clean and white – slightly damp with sap, that was all.

I was filled with relief. Pain without blood. Ideas started running through my head. I had never been able to do anything against pain before, compromised as I was by my reluctant pleasure at the sight of blood. But I could deal with this bloodless pain, because there was nothing to temper my horror of its cruelty. I would start a – well, I would do something to mitigate the suffering plants were forced to undergo.

I looked at the branch and gently caressed it, muttering – poor branch, it's all over now. Suddenly I felt self-conscious standing there, and, hiding the branch under my coat, hurried to the edge of the park and buried it beneath some fallen leaves.

By the time I got home, I had decided what I was going to

126

do. I rushed in to get some money, went to the little hardware shop across the road, and bought two plastic tubs. They were about two feet high, and as wide across, good enough for my purpose. I put one inside the other, and went back to the park. I had bought a little spade as well, it wasn't much use, looking more like one a child would use on a beach than anything else, but it would do.

I slipped through the park gates. It was nearly dusk, and there was no one else about. I went to one of the flower beds, and started to dig, taking great care to choose a bit of earth well away from the shrubs and rose bushes. The roses had come late that year, and the cloying scent of their flowers hung around me as I worked. Once I stood up clumsily to rest my back, and knocked one of the bushes. Petals fluttered to the ground. I stared at the seedhead with a vague kind of horror, and became aware of footsteps behind me.

I didn't like to turn round. I had read in the local paper about the perverts who haunt deserted places after dark. I was still holding the spade, but did not think it would be very effective even if I could bring myself to use it. So at last I turned round, ever so slowly, and found myself staring at the park-keeper, not more than three feet away from me, gripping one of those spikes which he uses for picking up dead leaves and bits of rubbish that people have dropped during the day.

I could tell he was the park-keeper, because he was wearing a uniform. But somehow I couldn't keep my eyes away from that spike he was holding in his hands. A moment ago it had been a tool, an impractical means of doing a boring job, as the few sweet-wrappers half-heartedly impaled there bore witness. I let my eyes travel up the path. There was lots more rubbish lying about. Then I looked back to the spike. His hands were clenched tightly round the metal, and from the way he held it alertly across his body, I knew that he now regarded it as a weapon, a possible means of defence against the intruder he'd noticed a moment ago, standing up suddenly among the flower beds. I dropped my plastic spade, which hardly made a sound as it hit the earth, and stood there, hands by my sides, waiting perhaps for him to produce a torch and flash it into my eyes.

He relaxed visibly when I dropped the spade, and tilted the spike to a slightly less threatening angle.

'Suppose you put those plants you've stolen right back where you got them from.'

I told him that I hadn't stolen anything; that I only wanted a little earth to put in the tubs that he could see beside me. He took one hand off the spike and played his torch over the scene – the two tubs standing awkwardly beside piles of upturned earth, gleaming wet and dark in the light.

'Why do you want it?'

I couldn't reply. I shook my head slightly, and muttered something about wanting it to put things in.

'What things?'

I tipped the earth out of the tubs and stacked them together. He seemed to gain confidence from my confusion, and planting the spike point down in the grass beside him, took out his torch again and played it over my face. I thought I had better be going, picked the tubs up in one hand, and found him standing in my way.

'Tell me what you were doing,' he said, and stepped in front of me again as I swerved to avoid him. I can't remember what I said – something about it being my business, and asking him to get out of my way.

'I think I could take you in for wilful damage of property,' he said, and I glanced behind me at the heaps of earth. I hadn't hurt anything, and protested. 'There's that flower,' he said, pointing, 'and don't try to run,' when I made as if to, 'because I've already shut the gates.'

I suspected this was a bluff, and turned on him, asking why he should harass me in this way. All my alarm and embarrassment at being caught went into pure anger. As I ran at him, he spread his arms wide to catch me, but I ducked and made a grab for the spike behind him. His face whitened, and he dragged me back just as I grasped it. It fell to the ground, and as he stepped back to kick it out of my reach, I broke free, and with the tubs tucked under one arm, made for the gate. It wasn't locked. I ran down the street and ducked into a shop doorway. He didn't follow me, and after that, I never went into the park again. There was a patch of waste ground, quite near my house where I could dig as much earth as I liked and no one would ever notice. But sometimes I go past the edge of the park in the evening, and when I pass his house I stare through the window, and think very hard about him. The light's on by then, and I can usually see the glow of a television, and sometimes a dark shape outlined against a chair, because he doesn't close the curtains. What would occur to him if he knew I was looking through the window, thinking of that moment I touched the spike, and could have killed him, from blind rage, with no regard for the pain?

I don't allow myself to think about it very often. Most of the time I just concentrate on rescuing plants.

My biggest problem is that the room where I live has no fit place for me to put my vegetables when I can no longer keep them alive in pots of water on the window sill. All the cups and dishes have their special plants. Lettuces are my favourite, but it seems they're the most delicate of all. Sometimes I stroke them, they're so beautiful that I really can't resist it, but I shouldn't, because they don't like it. So I look at them instead, and study each droop and curl of the leaf, every vibrant vein. I talk to them, but they prefer music, so I leave the radio on very quietly when I go out. Although I persevere, and try to look after them as best I can, they always wither. It's too late when I get to them. When I go past gardens which have been neglected, I see them bolted and seeding all over the place, and it consoles me to know that even ones which aren't cut can't be kept alive indefinitely. But the problem of burial – for although the floorboards are wood I don't think it would be very nice to put them down there – is one which always bothers me. So in the plastic tubs which I use, I try to create an environment where vegetable matter can rest peacefully.

I have devised my own ritual of burial, which takes place weekly when all the dead vegetables are placed neatly in the tub, and a thin covering of earth is applied and patted down with a trowel. I made some bad mistakes at first, and buried vegetables which weren't quite ready. They still contained moisture, and their rotting under the earth produced an appalling smell. I had to drag that tub out, late at night, and haul it all the way to the waste ground, where I tipped it into a hole. Now I take them out of water after a week, and leave them to dry on the sill for another ten days until they are quite dessicated. This prevents them composting so quickly, which is what happened the first time.

I read about this in a book I took from a bookshop – but I feel a bit bad about books, which is why I don't read novels any more, and before I got very far in I felt ashamed of what I was doing, and put the book in a bucket of water, where it could return to something resembling its natural state. When it had been there for three weeks mould started to grow. I took this as a sign that it was gradually approaching a state nearer to the tree it had once been – for although mould's a poor substitute for moss, I think it grows for the same reasons, on the north side of the tree which is cold and damp like the bucket of water. And mould can be so pretty sometimes. This was quite dull and white, but there was an awful lot of it. So I gave the book a proper burial in one of the tubs.

Sometimes I'm quite astonished by how far I've come. When I think back to the first day, and my strange sympathy with the tree's pain – well, I'm sure that at that moment not one hundredth of the things that I do now occurred to me. It seems to have been a very gradual process. I realised, quite quickly of course, that I must stop eating vegetables – but that was only a moral gesture. After all, the vegetables would have experienced pain – even death of a sort – long before I would have had anything to do with them. And I had no illusions that my ceasing to eat vegetables would save even one carrot from being plucked and packaged. At first I could have become depressed, for it seemed I was the only person who had realised, or was ever likely to realise, that plants felt pain; and if I told people what I had discovered, it seemed unlikely that they would believe me, or that even if they did, that they would care very much. I was alone, and loneliness is depressing. But I soon discovered a different kind of companionship. I surrounded myself with more and more plants, haunting each florist's and chainstore that sold them, bringing home as many as I could afford. Their sympathetic presence reassured me, and eased my frustration.

Yet sometimes I still felt lonely, though to admit it seemed like a kind of treachery to them. That's when I started my daily visits to the supermarket, picking out the vegetables which had the best chance of being sustained a little longer. At least I was saving them from the indignity of being eaten. While I'm there, I observe people closely – that's what I was doing at the beginning of the diary – and watching them in this strange place, where their behaviour is exaggerated by the odd conditions of light, temperature, and confusion, helps to dull my longing for human contact for the day.

And now I have reached the stage where I even feel guilty writing this. The paper on which I'm writing came from a tree. When I think about that tree being sawed up, I feel sick and faint. But I will continue. Writing all this may help me. When I have finished – at some as yet to be defined point – I will tear it up, and put the pieces in a bucket of water. Then once it's broken down, and fairly dry, I will be able to bury it in one of the tubs.

I shall look forward to that day. But I don't know how to finish the diary – I can't just stop. If one day I leave it, I would be back to it the next – in spite of what I've just said, it would be impossible to destroy it. And yet, as I go on, it seems to create more problems than it solves. Writing down all my feelings seems to intensify them. There is no gradual easing of frustration, no gentle exorcism, as I had hoped. It just makes things worse. What I write about the blood – it brings it back to me, as I'd never felt it since that day. And the park-keeper's spike, which he balanced so skillfully between his hands – it is like torture to recall it. And this loneliness, nagging at me each day in this curiously dulled state, is worst of all. I feel as if it is driving me to kill someone.

Perhaps that would be a way out of it. I'm not sure if it would be a very good one – afterwards things might be worse than they are now – or they might be cured. If, just once, I could see blood flow, knowing that it had come by my own hand – my fascination might be purged, my fear of causing pain quieted, so that I wouldn't be so afraid. I am naturally appalled at the thought of murder, but it seems that the more I struggle against it, the more tempting it becomes. It is not even the thought of the flowing blood: just the possibility of release from the conflicting tensions that torment me. It doesn't matter who I kill – as long as I am not found out. It couldn't be anyone I knew, it would have to be a stranger in a public place. It doesn't matter where, as long as no one sees. There are plenty of public places which are often deserted.

But how should I go about it? I envisaged myself, waiting, with a knife in my pocket – it would have to be a knife – behind bushes, in a deserted street, to select the first person that came along. My head was throbbing. I poured myself a glass of water and tried to think straight. Even an apparently deserted place was usually within earshot of someone. And since I would be using a knife, my victim might make a great deal of noise. Trying to think of any place on the human body where a wound would be instantly fatal, I felt a sick revulsion at the thought of causing pain sweep through me. Yet even as I write it is turning to mounting excitement. I could not think of one, and it struck me that as my hands would probably be trembling, it was quite irrelevant. If I missed a particular spot, I might be so upset at my plan going wrong that I'd lose my head altogether. Then what would I do about the knife? Once I'd stabbed my victim, I would have to pull it out, and again I worried about the state I might be in and whether I would be about to do this. I drank another glass of water and my hands were really trembling. I can hardly manage to write this at all.

So there are several points to consider. The murder will be a climactic act which will allow me to stop writing and destroy this diary. It may help me.

The murder must be in a public place, unable to be seen or heard from anywhere else. This suggests somewhere enclosed. I couldn't think of a way round this – until it occurred to me that the enclosed place need not necessarily be remote. It struck me that as long as no one could actually see in, there would be a positive advantage in somewhere really busy. If there was lots of noise all around it, any little sounds my murder might involve would go unnoticed.

I almost gave up. It was too difficult, too risky, the likelihood of being caught was so high – and then I started to think about my victim. I decided not to focus on a particular type, but to see what came into my head. Would it be he or she? Old or young? Fair-haired or dark; wearing glasses; bearded. Or dressed in blue, green stripes – a scarf, high-heeled shoes, carrying a bag? I would never know more about them than their physical appearance. What a way to decide the prolonging or curtailing of someone's life – depending on the colour of shoes they had put on that morning. Perhaps I should go to a particular place, pick the first person with black slip-on shoes, and follow them, waiting for an opportunity to kill them.

But I rejected this method. Then I thought that perhaps I ought to be humane. I could walk into a hospital, and kill someone that was dying anyway. But then I thought that there wouldn't be any point in that. And I would be almost certain to be caught. I could hardly even plead a mercy killing, since the kind of messy knife wound that I was likely to inflict would hardly be a kindness to anyone. And being in a hospital, my victim, moribund though he or she already was, might even be patched up. It really was a very bad idea. But for some reason the whole thing struck me as funny, and I began to laugh.

It was warmer, though. I would choose a place – somewhere like a hospital – large and bustling where no one is too sure what is going on. Suddenly it occurred to me that the supermarket, where I went every day, would be the perfect place to commit a murder. I shut my eyes and tried to visualise those long straight rows of shelves, higher than a human head, those long narrow alleyways where two trollies could not pass. It could not be there, of course. I leant back in my chair, and let my mind travel up one of those alleys, past tins of soup and milk. At the end, set back in the wall, was a white door that said in red letters 'STAFF ONLY'.

I had seen people going in and out of this door, carrying

boxes, or pushing great trollies loaded with tins. I had peered through it, at these moments, and as far as I could see, it led into a plain corridor floored and tiled with white from which other doors opened into what I took to be storerooms. Could I just walk in there and kill the first person I saw?

Surely I would be stopped if I just tried to walk in. I needed an excuse, a pretext which would render me invisible, for if there appeared to be some reason for my entering the storerooms, no one would ever notice me. I could pretend to be delivering something – deliveries usually went in round the back – but I could say that someone had forgotten something, or that it had been put in the wrong consignment and I'd just found it. I could always act stupid, if they weren't convinced. But with such a lot of things happening, would anyone really care? I would walk in with my box – easy enough to get an empty box from somewhere. I could pack it up to a decent weight, and reseal it with wide tape. It would be a good enough excuse. I would go in at a busy time – slightly later than usual – at lunchtime – and choose the most helpless assistant to help me with my box. I would follow them into the store room, and as soon as an opportunity presented itself, I would kill them. Then I could dump my box and leave. Perhaps I could put another coat in the box, to put on over my other clothes when I left in case there was any blood.

The weapon was still a problem. But when I found a box which had contained some form of processed chicken, I remembered how when I looked through butchers' windows, there were all those great knives inside, and an uncomfortable excitement took hold of me as I thought of the deadly implements which the butchering section of a supermarket might contain. I would take my chance. I thought again about the park-keeper's spike and what a beautiful weapon that made.

'I wonder,' I said aloud, 'if I had killed him, would I have been found out?'

I visualised his body, stretched out along those mounds of earth that I'd disturbed, some of the petals from the fallen rose entangled in his hair, meshed down in the mud, his cap nowhere to be seen, his mouth open. And the proud spear of the spike sticking through his body, glinting slightly in the light from his fallen torch.

I walked over to the window, and shivered. The night felt cold, and I drew the curtains to protect the plants from frost.

'Perhaps,' I said to them, 'tomorrow I will be a murderer.'

I touched their leaves. The thought made me warm inside, but my hands trembled. Palms upwards, I stared at them: thinking of all the blood that might flow across them tomorrow. I wished to inflict a deep wound, so deep that it would bleed for a long time. If I could prevent it from clotting, I would do so. My knees started to shake, and I sat down on the floor. Didn't I care about inflicting pain anymore?

'It will be so sudden,' I said aloud, 'that there won't be any pain.'

And I groaned. It seemed too simple and inevitable. How could I live, knowing that I had killed someone? Somehow it didn't matter. But I knew it ought to matter, I got up and tried to make myself some toast. I took the bag out from under the sink, but when my fingers tried to pick up the bread they couldn't hold it. Its slightly damp feel disgusted me. I dropped the slices on the floor, and let them lie. Then I attempted to pour myself another glass of water, and broke the glass. I picked up a piece of glass and tried to draw it across my wrist. But I couldn't. I burst out sobbing and fell asleep on the floor.

When I woke, it was light. I lay there for a moment until all that had happened came back to me. Then I turned over on my face and groaned. Eventually, deciding that I could not go back to sleep and blot it all out, I got up, and had a bath, which did something to clear my head.

It occurred to me that I could not go back now, because I did not want to. I felt curiously numb. Causing pain, and the sight of blood, which had seemed so important to me the day before, no longer mattered. I had resolved to commit murder.

But I would have to postpone it until I was sure exactly how to do it. My idea of the night before seemed rather naïve. It occurred to me that all the people I had ever seen delivering or collecting things at the supermarket were in some kind of uniform – that of the delivery firm, or of the company. There was no way that I could imitate one of these. I settled down to think it over. My original plan was too difficult, and insufficiently worked out. I needed something which was less likely to go wrong.

And I remembered that all the staff at the supermarket had name badges on their overalls. So that if I memorised a name, waited until that person went for their lunchbreak, then walked up to one of the other staff and asked for them – I was bound to be let in through that door. Again, that was too complicated. I could just wait until that person went through, make my own way past the door, and if anyone stopped and challenged me I would have this person's name at the ready. But then they might take me to the person I was asking for. A false name would be better, one quite like one of the real ones. If there was really a Mrs Mackie, I could ask for Mrs McKay, and if things became difficult, I could falter and pretend to have come to the wrong place. If I carried no weapon, there would be nothing to incriminate me.

I would have to chance it. With luck, I would be able to get right into the recesses of the storerooms without being challenged. I figured that the butchering section would be quite deserted by lunchtime. Most of the cutting up of the meat would be done in the early morning, before the shop opened. Perhaps there would be one person there, cleaning up, but I thought it more likely that there would be no one there at all. So where was my victim? There was no point in making all these preparations if I could not be sure that there would actually be someone to kill.

This was a problem which I could not solve without further research. So, after a leisurely breakfast, I went out to the supermarket, somewhat after my usual time.

It was very crowded. I picked up a wire basket, quite mechanically, and let myself be carried along on the rush of people. Everything was more confused than usual, and after a while I worked out that they were moving everything around. The signs indicating different kinds of produce had been stripped down, in their places were just wire frames with empty pegs. I remembered now that I had seen the notices about store changes, but had not been aware of the dates.

Everyone around me was confused. As hands picked goods off the shelves, hesitated, and finally placed them in the baskets, the lights seemed unbearably bright. I shut my eyes, and stood for a moment, letting people push past me, feeling dizzy, as elbows and trollies jostled me for a second before passing on. The empty wire basket at my feet was kicked away from me. Then I opened my eyes. Someone was apologising, someone else cursing me for 'standing there like an idiot'. I left my basket where it had slid, under some shelves, and wandered on through the tide of people.

I came to the 'STAFF ONLY' door, looked round to make sure no one was watching, and pushed it open. It swung shut behind me. I walked, as calmly as possible, up the corridor, counting the doors that I passed. There were three rooms which appeared to be empty, except for some boxes, then the corridor turned right, through a pair of swing doors. On the left was an office of some kind where I could see a woman's back through the glass panel of the door. Two steps on, to the right, was what looked like a filing cabinet. And at the end of the corridor, through another pair of swing doors, I saw the gleam of steel counters, and the endless rows of large hooks, suspended from the ceiling.

I heard the click of the office door and dodged behind the cabinet. But the woman couldn't have seen me, for I heard her steps going off in the opposite direction. The swing doors swished, and I was alone.

Walking cautiously up to the other doors, I gave one a gentle push. It wasn't locked. Then I breathed in, and looked around. There was no one there. I went in, very slowly, almost expecting to be challenged by someone I couldn't see. But I wasn't. I had the place entirely to myself, and could inspect what was to be the site of my murder.

There were three long counters, made of steel. Each had a sink at one end. Above these counters hung the hooks. Along the walls, there were cupboards. These, as I suspected, were locked. I guessed they contained the knives, and contemplated running to the woman's office, in the hope that it was left unlocked, and rummaging for the keys in the hope that one of them opened these cupboards. Then I laughed shakily. I would have to be careful. The way I was going, I was liable to be caught. It was risky enough just being here.

I decided to look round one last time, and if there was nothing suitable for my purpose, to forget the whole idea. But the thought of giving it up made me panic, and, as I stood there, my hands began to shake and my mouth went dry, so that I would have been unable to speak if there had been anyone to speak to. It was while I was standing so, totally unable to think how to continue or abandon my plan, that I heard footsteps coming down the corridor.

At first I thought it was the woman coming back. In that case I was safe, she would turn into her office. But the steps weren't like hers, they were heavier, and yet more nervous. They were the steps of a very young man. My body started to work again and I slid down behind one of the counters at the far end of the room.

The steps paused. Obviously he was carrying something and had stopped to readjust it. He must be just behind the door. I had a last chance to change my position, and hardly knew what I was doing as I shuffled along behind the counter on my hands and knees so that I was nearer, yet still well out of sight – unless he looked too closely – of the knife cupboard.

But would he open the cupboard? I was no longer afraid of discovery. I had had no chance to select my victim, but here he was – and if he once opened that cupboard, and I could get to a knife, he was surely done for. It was unbearably exciting. My pulse was going twice as fast as usual, and as I heard the swing doors open, I made myself small in my hiding place and craned my neck so that I could see him.

I could only see his back. He was using it to open the door, as he dragged the trolley in after him. I could not see what was on the trolley. If it was packaged meat my plan must fail. But if it was something he had to cut – the trolley was in full view now.

It was piled with boxes which he began to unload. It would take him several minutes, and when he was finished, I would be able to go. There would be no murder.

Then I felt terribly weak, It was not going to work, and I would be left with these tensions which I was unable to ease. Tears welled up in my eyes. How I wanted to kill him! And as yet I had only seen his back, and didn't even know if I would recognise him for someone I had seen before, loading things onto the shelves in the shop. I wiped my eyes on the back of my hand and tried to study his back. Narrow shoulders, rather narrow hips under the close fitting coat. The coat was white, and I could see where his shirt tucked into his trousers underneath. The counter prevented me from seeing his legs. Hair – an odd sort of ginger, quite greasy, which already looked as if it was starting to grey. A pang shot through me. All this told me nothing, except that he might not be as young as I'd thought. But what did it matter? He was not going to be my victim, after all.

Suddenly steps were approaching down the corridor. I recognised them as the woman's. Surely they would stop at her office. But no, they continued, and a moment later the movement of the swing doors told me that she had come in.

'Stephen, why are you putting these boxes here? I told you to put them in the storeroom.'

His reply was mumbled. I guess it was something about the storeroom being full, or disorganised, and how he'd been told by someone else to bring them here.

'But he knows it's not suitable here for this kind of goods.'

This was obviously directed against the someone else and was followed by an exasperated sigh.

'All right, I'll go and sort him out. You can leave these here for the moment. Take them all off the trolley – and perhaps you'd better open up a box to check that they've sent us the right order. We've had trouble with them before.'

He mumbled something else.

'Here, take my scissors. You can drop them back in my office when you've finished.'

The doors banged together as she went out. The footsteps did not stop at her office, but carried on beyond the second pair of doors. Stephen and I were alone.

What could I do? Could I get him to turn round? Should I leap on him from behind and try to get the scissors out of his hand? I remembered the park-keeper, and how he had held the spike across his body. Would this young man do the same with the scissors if I stood up to accost him? I contemplated calling out his name, 'Stephen!' to see what he would do. But this would put him immediately on his guard, and he might run for the door, which was exactly what I didn't want. I had to think.

He was almost finished with the boxes, when I realised that he wasn't holding the scissors. I looked around, but could not see them anywhere, and surmised that they must be in the pocket of his overall. So I couldn't really take him by surprise. either.

Suddenly, working from a blind impulse, I stood up, as quietly as possible, with my back to him. I didn't make much noise, but I was stiff from crouching, and he may have heard something. Of course, I couldn't see his reaction. I stood there, quite still. If he didn't see me, he was quite safe – but I did not see how he could fail to notice me.

I don't know how long it was before the rhythmical motion of stacking the boxes ceased. But it seemed as if there was a sudden fear in the air – not straightforward alarm, but mixed with a little curiosity. If he panicked and made for the door, I would remain here. Anyone he summoned would find me standing quite still, with no weapon anywhere to be seen. There would be nothing to prove against me. But he was not going to run away. He was coming up behind me.

'What are you doing?'

His voice was very small and timid. I didn't reply.

'You shouldn't be here without authorisation.'

After a pause, he said, 'I'll have to fetch someone.'

At this I turned round, moved a few steps backwards, and smiled, which made him uneasy enough to reach into his pocket for the scissors. I reacted as if they frightened me.

'Please...'

'Are you a customer?'

I nodded. After toying with the scissors for a moment, he

140

put them down rather self-consciously on the counter beside him. 'Then what are you doing here?'

I shook my head and moved towards him, gesticulating as if for help. He said that he'd really have to fetch someone, and at the moment he turned, my fingers reached for the scissors and plunged them into his side. He gasped, and tried to run, but I caught him round the waist and stabbed him again and again until he fell on the floor. There was an awful lot of blood all over my hands when eventually I pulled the scissors free and stood there, breathing deeply, over my victim. My head felt wonderfully clear. I had not panicked. There had been very little noise: after his first gasp, the only sound was that of the falling body.

Now I had to act quickly. I went to one of the sinks and turned the cold tap on full, letting it run over my hands and the part of my sleeve where the blood had splashed. It was wonderful how easily it came off. My sleeve looked wet, but it would pass. Fortunately there was no blood on the rest of me. Then I washed the scissors, and dried them meticulously on Stephen's coat. Stephen himself I dragged out of sight behind the counter. Finally I washed my face, which felt very flushed, picked up the scissors with the end of my dry sleeve, and walked out through the swing doors.

The woman had not yet returned to her office, so I put the scissors on her desk. I had been careful to leave no finger prints when I dried them on Stephen's coat, so the only prints they would have would belong to the first person who picked them up. I did not want to incriminate anyone else, but I was quite determined not to be caught. I had to wait behind the swing doors while a loaded trolley went past, but was able to slip out into the corridor, and into the shop, without being seen. I mingled with the customers, as many as ever, and fought my way back through the crowd to the place where I had left my basket. I retrieved it, put in three items at random, paid for them in a dream, and left the supermarket.

Goldtown

One

It was the bleakest place he'd ever seen: snow piled on either side of the perimeter fence, the outline of buildings in the fading light, and the faint noise of the plane that had brought him here taking off into the dull sky. The air was too cold to let him shiver. He hunched his shoulders instinctively inside his coat and turned to the driver of the truck standing beside him.

– You said you know where my mother lives?

– Downstairs from me.

The driver of the truck was young, fair, blade-thin. The skin round his eyes was screwed up prematurely from looking at the snow glare. The eyes were pale blue, opaque.

– My wife's having a baby, he added as they climbed into the truck. – Your mother's looking after her.

The stranger smiled as if this amused him. The truck smelt of the oranges that lay, packed in shallow crates, beneath the tarpaulin at the back.

– How much do you sell these for?

The truck driver seemed to hesitate before replying

– What people will pay for them.

The rebuke in his voice wasn't very confident. He made a noise in his throat, changing gear, then added,

– People go crazy for fresh food round here.

– Anything to make a change, said the stranger, stretching out. – Does everything get brought in from outside?

The driver took his eyes off the road for a minute.

– No-o, he said, in a voice that seemed much too startled. The colour in his face changed, through embarrassment or panic.

– We keep chickens.

– You do? said the stranger, smiling. Something in his tone

142

seemed to upset the driver, who looked up at him covertly.

– Do you own the store? asked the stranger, hardly bothering to notice.

– No, I just work there.

His voice had altered again. Off the subject of himself, it became dull and even.

Both were relieved when they drew up outside the store. It was a big building, lit with globes along the front that gave a weird colour to the top of the pale-blue sign.

– Your mother lives just round the corner, said the driver. His hands lay loosely on the wheel.

As the stranger climbed out, he saw a figure outlined against the yellow light of the doorway. It seemed to hesitate on catching sight of him, then the door swung shut and it was just another blur in the snow.

The shock of the wind driving at his face forced his eyes shut. He put up his hands instinctively to shield them but the freezing air cut through his gloves, partially thawed in the truck and now resetting into ice. He had an impression of solid walls in the whirling snow, punctured by slits of ice far up. As he groped his way round the corner, the wind lessened, and he found himself in a covered alley, created by the roofs on either side sloping down.

For a moment he stood quite still, his face unreadable in the dark. Then he raised his hand, and knocked.

– Jackson, his mother said, when she opened the door.

He didn't speak. Her shock was too pure to allow her to be surprised. All she could think about was how he'd changed.

– Can I come in?

As she nodded dumbly and moved back, he shut the door behind him and the passage seemed suddenly quiet.

– I thought I'd never see you again.

He laughed uncomfortably.

– Come inside and get warm.

He didn't quite know what to do with himself as she led the way into the single, big room that comprised her flat. They halted awkwardly in the centre for a moment, then she turned away and opened the stove door to make it burn more brightly. She could feel him looking about the room. A slight anticipation of panic forced her to swallow, then looking round at him, she said abruptly.

– Pat's not here.

His eyes caught hers for a moment.

– I didn't expect him to be.

She tried to memorise the look of his face as he said that.

– He left four months ago.

There was something guarded in her tone. As she glanced up, he thought she'd managed to take his reappearance remarkably well.

– I came to see you, he said, conscious that he avoided any warmth.

She made a slight self-conscious movement. – How did you find me?

He smiled for the first time. – It's not that difficult. You'd know, if you tried.

The room was warm and peaceful. A bucket of water set by the stove steamed slightly. Jackson looked round again at the two corners curtained off with unbleached calico, the cupboard stacked with plates, the table and two chairs.

– Can I stay?

His smile annoyed her. For a moment she thought – Why should he? but her nod came automatically. She knew from his expression that he wasn't going to tell her any more.

– Would you like something to eat? she asked abruptly.

He nodded. She was angry with herself. As she turned away he made an effort to isolate her from the events they both had in mind.

– Ann, he said quietly.

She stiffened. It had always annoyed her when he used her name but it wasn't meant to now.

– What?

Something in his face changed.

– I've got nothing to apologise for.

Two

It was a summer night, strangely perfect in his recollection. He sometimes wondered if it were ever possible to forget such things, then thought, with a sharper sense of pain, that the image which recurred so frequently was only a compounded fantasy of the emotions he'd felt since.

He lay on the narrow couch where his mother saw her patients, staring at the red glow of the stove diffused through the off-white curtain. The couch was hard. He didn't know how long he'd been lying like that, unable to get deeper than a doze. As he squeezed his eyes tightly shut, the itch all over him seemed to resolve itself into a specifically sexual urge. His face was as expressionless as a sleeper's. He rolled carefully onto his face, putting his arms up above his head.

He felt it was the warmth of the night that had betrayed him. He remembered lying naked on his bed, staring up through the open window. Scents of the garden drifted in. There was a faint hum of insect life, varying with the breeze.

He remembered looking at the three-quarters moon, wondering why it sometimes missed the top, sometimes the bottom. He was physically very conscious of its light on him; it spilled over onto the sheet and throughout the room. There was a patch of sweat under his back. As he wriggled against it, he was intensely aware of contact.

He spread his palms wide on either side of his body, experiencing a strange excitement as he thought of what his touch encompassed. He started to recite to himself – my hand touch the sheet, the sheet the bed, the bed the floor, then the room, the house, street, town, country, sea, air. I am physically linked to these things. Every bird, fish, every other person is somehow connected to me.

He opened his eyes and turned his head at a noise outside. The door was open for any cool draught. He had a physically intense image of Pat, standing in the doorway looking at him. Pat was wearing a shirt with wide blue stripes. The moonlight paled out his tan, reducing his body to architectural planes.

– Couldn't you sleep?

Pat shook his head.

– Me neither.

Jackson felt he ought to move but didn't want to.

– It's too hot, said Pat.

He remained in the doorway. Jackson rolled over on his side. The ticking of a clock on the table beside his bed irritated him; reaching up, he snapped it into its case and placed it in the drawer. Pat smiled.

– Why did you do that?

– Don't know, said Jackson. He stared at Pat, then for a moment, looked away.

– Why don't you come out?

– I'm tired.

– Your mother's got some beer downstairs. We could get some cake, go down by the river.

Jackson fixed his eyes on the pillow a few inches below his face. Then he sank his head into it, biting as widely as his mouth permitted.

– What's the matter?

He made an effort as if to roll over with the pillow still in his teeth, then laughed and came free. He was lying on his back, staring up at Pat's face. He put his right hand over the wet place where his mouth had been.

– Pat.

His eyes widened. Jackson meant to smile, but his face stayed stiff. As slowly Pat sank down on the bed beside him, his face didn't change. Pat sat still for a moment, as if reflecting, then turned and put his hand on Jackson's stomach. Jackson blinked, feeling the individual pressure of the fingers. Then their eyes met.

He remembered how terrified Pat looked. An extraordinary sense of pleasure was filling him, yet drifting to the top of his mind was the concern that Pat should enjoy it too. When he tried to form his name, it was inaudible. The dark eyes in the chalk-white face burned down at him. In a moment his limbs relaxed and he was able to reach up and take him in his arms.

He lay rigidly still on the narrow couch, his hands folded cross-wise over his stomach. The light in the stove had dimin-

146

ished until it just coloured the darkness.

His face was a mask which suggested expressions without anything of what had gone to make them. For a while his eyes stared and blinked, then at last he shut them tight and rolled over as if he didn't want to look at the dark anymore.

Three

She watched him pour a second cup of coffee.

– You should go and take a look around.

As he stared across at her she read his look almost as an accusation. It irritated rather than alarmed her. She rose to clear away the plates while he still sat there, sipping from an old blue cup with cracked glaze that she knew he remembered from their old house.

– Have you got people coming?

She nodded, annoyed that her movements seemed jerky and febrile. As he got up, putting the cup down on the table, she reached for it, meeting his fingers half-way round where they had failed to let go. For a moment it swayed, then coffee was soaking into the pale wood. She released it with an exaggerated gesture. It slipped from his fingers with a crash, and he met her eyes with faint disbelief as they stared at the blue shards that littered the floor around his feet.

– Oh, Jackson! was all she said.

As he started to pick up the fragments she got out a coat and a pair of boots from behind the curtain in the corner.

– You'll need these.

– He didn't get any fatter, he remarked as he put them on.

– Thanks.

A slight smile reinforced the irony in his voice.

For a moment after he went out she felt she couldn't move. Her face was practically fleshless, set into a parody of itself. Her eyes ranged the room, as if she was trying to locate something. Her lips moved slightly. Then her face cleared, becoming serious.

He found the layout of the town strangely appealing. It would never shed the marks of its origin: there was something

147

feverish about it. Everywhere had been turned up at one time. Strange mounds under the snow indicated abandoned workings, scratched higgledy-piggledy in spurts of activity that had ceased abruptly when disillusionment set in. Buildings fronted every way as if no one had ever decided where the streets ought to be. Here and there he saw things that amused him. Some shacks had been added to, given a coat of paint and fancy trimmings that highlighted their essential shoddiness. One front was framed by a verandah, meticulously sculpted out of hammered tin. Its scalloped border was enhanced by the clustering icicles that broke and dripped in the diffused, strangely underwater light of the morning sun.

He leaned against the wall for a moment to watch this, then the wall itself caught his attention. It was smooth and flush, as if professionally built, crowned by a solid-looking roof three feet above his head. As he eyes took this in, he became aware of faint sounds of movement on the other side.

– Do you want to see inside?

He spun round with a sense of shock as the voice echoed his thoughts.

The speaker was, he guessed, seven or eight months pregnant. She wore a red coat which just fitted over her stomach.

– I've just been feeding them, she went on. – You're welcome to take a look, they won't notice.

He didn't quite know why he agreed. She led him round the building to a door.

– In here.

As she banged down the bolt and flung the door wide, a light came on, illuminating hundreds of eyes. They were all near the floor, crouched down on a deep litter. As the door swung shut a raucous cackling went up.

– I hate them. When the seabirds come overhead, in summer, they go wild.

She laughed to herself, not registering his reaction.

– Look at these.

She pointed at two containers standing in the snow. They were filled with small blueish almost perfect spheres. When he realised they were eggs, he felt a kind of amused disgust. Her face was quietly furious; he had the impression he'd strayed in on some deep resentment.

As she met his eyes a bitter smile spread across her face. She stretched her hands out upon the red cloth that covered her stomach.

– How do you think it feels, she said quietly – to know there's something wrong inside?

Four

He had a suddenly brutal memory of his father's funeral.

The sky was a very deep blue. He lay in the grass, looking up, until he felt that the light was dissolving him away. He closed his eyes, very relaxed, as he'd drunk a whole bottle of wine before lying down.

A giggle escaped him into the grass.

– What more do you want, Pat?

He flung out one arm, enjoying the delirious loss of control. Then he rolled his body loosely along the earth, into the shade of a tree. He saw a bird overhead as a blur against the coloured light.

– Silly thing.

He imagined it looking at him. Then he was holding his mother's hand beside the grave, sniffing the wet earth that reminded him of medicine. Disturbed by a sudden noise, he looked up, and saw his mother's glove splitting from end to end of her palm.

He forced his knees up into the air and considered his own death. The glimpse of his mother's face behind the veil seemed to end mystification. He had a drunkenly romantic presentiment that she would outlive him.

– She's absorbed everything else in my life.

He brought his hands up, slowly, so he was looking through splayed fingers. The image of his mother with Pat, translated through the perspective of his own jealousy, attacked him.

He had a vision of suicide, his own choked face cut off by a cord at the neck. For a moment the heady idea of inflicting

149

guilt possessed him.

He let his heels slide through the grass, ripping up its roots. Then he was aware of someone calling his name. In the silence that followed, a shadow blotted out the light above him.

– What are you doing here?

Pat was older, dressed differently. He squatted on the ground beside Jackson, awkwardly avoiding any contact.

– You don't even get one guess.

Jackson smiled tiredly as he spoke. Defiance was the only enjoyable thing left.

On Pat's face was a curious mixture of resentment and regret. He looked away abruptly, seeming to grow absorbed in restlessly tearing up the grass between his fingers.

– Have you asked her if she dreams about you?

Pat's face grew suddenly sharp.

– I dream about you.

He felt he could say it, lying there half-drunk in the grass. He'd shut his eyes to protect himself from Pat's reaction. When he opened them again, Pat had gone.

Five

Night fell on the still plateau.

He lay awake listening to his mother's short, troubled breathing. Every now and then came a low noise as if she was talking to herself.

He hardly dared move for fear of waking her. Then there came a hiss and crackle from the stove. As he turned his head, a shadow loomed on the opposite curtain. In a minute she emerged, an old coat wrapped over her nightdress.

– Go to sleep, she said when she saw him.

He didn't say anything, just looked at her. As he lay still on the bed, she came across and sat beside him.

– Go to sleep, Jackson.

Her fingers were cold as they reached out to touch his head. He closed his eyes. Neither of them spoke. He made his breathing easy, conscious of her attention relapsing and focussing again as the pressure of her fingers varied in stroking his head.

He was gradually aware that she was listening. Into the silence of their breathing came a new sound, muffled, but not far off.

– What is it? he said with his eyes still closed.

She knew he hadn't been asleep.

– Our neighbours.

– What's the matter?

She bent over him a little more.

– Go to sleep.

Her voice teased and soothed him. He was aware of the fire glow pricking behind his lids, then the slow movement with which his mother got up off the bed and left him.

When, with a sudden shock, he awoke, the room was thrillingly quiet. He waited till he was sure she was asleep, then stood up, as quietly as he could on the couch, raising his eyes to the ceiling overhead. There were sounds as if someone was walking restlessly above, and the small irritable noises of displacement that indicated they were doing something while their attention was elsewhere.

He imagined the girl and the young man. He shared their desperation, a curiously random fear of what the future held.

After he didn't know how long, he put on his clothes and went out.

The snow glittered with an extra hard frost which had put a fresh surface on the slush of the day before. As he stepped into the street, his breath froze around him and he bent his hands together inside his gloves in an effort to persuade them to be warm.

He was aware that someone else was about. After a minute, a figure came into view around a corner. It didn't hesitate on seeing him, but came towards him, stepping freely and swiftly through the snow. Quite close, it stopped, and he watched with fascination as the gloved hands went up to the head and started to unwind the folds of the hood that all but covered the face.

His Right Hand

One

The train wasn't very full, so you might have wondered why both the women standing in the corridor where two coaches joined chose to stay and compromise their privacy.

They were watching each other without seeming to. The one by the door had slid the glass down the tiniest crack, and every ten minutes she flicked another cigarette butt out into the snow that lay beyond the tracks outside. She was of medium height, stringy, with aggressively yellow hair shaved off close at the back of her neck. Her eyes were blue, and the skin of her face weathered, so lines were etched where there wasn't flesh for wrinkles to form. She looked about thirty. There was a large shabby grip between her feet which showed a patch of pristine leather where a name plate had been prised off.

The other woman smiled lazily. She said

– I know you've got a gun in that bag.

– So what if I have?

– I know of two jobs in town that might require one; I wondered which you were after.

The yellow-haired woman's eyes narrowed, then she inclined her head and smiled.

– I'm working at the carnival.

The other woman grinned. – You're not the police? Then I'll tell you all about myself.

– Look, said the yellow-haired woman sharply. – What is all this?

– I thought it unfair to have the advantage of you, Miss Gray. I saw your picture in the paper. I've got a good memory.

– I suppose you remember everything you read about me as well.

– I don't necessarily believe it. Oh don't look at me like

that. You can tell me later, when you've listened to what I want to say.

She paused.

– My name is Jenny Diver. I'm thirty-six years old and the most successful thief in this part of the world. I run the bar in the town we're both going to.

Phoebe shrugged.

– I want you to hold me up, said Jenny Diver.

Phoebe began to laugh. She shook her head.

– You'll be well paid.

– I've got a job.

– Ten thousand.

– Why so much?

– You aim well, Jenny smiled. She indicated the window. – While I've been watching you, you haven't missed one of those stubs.

– You want me to shoot you? Phoebe stared down at the bag between her feet.

– I want you to miss me, Jenny corrected. – Very convincingly.

She could see by the uncomfortable look on her face that Phoebe was tempted.

– Are you crazy? she said eventually, less convincingly.

– No, but I'm in some trouble.

Phoebe's cigarette dropped to the floor and she crushed it absently with her foot.

– Can you tell me why I should trust you, Jenny Diver?

– No.

Jenny seemed amused by the whole thing. – But you can contact me at the bar if you want to take it up.

– Ten thousand, echoed Phoebe thoughtfully.

– It would last you some time. Not for ever. But if you wanted to escape for a little while...

Jenny shrugged. – I do believe you're interested.

She leaned back against the partition, satisfied with the look of resentful admiration Phoebe gave her. She watched her with half-closed eyes, registering a slight indecision in her face that made her seem younger than she'd first appeared.

– I'm a sad freak, Phoebe began. She shrugged self-consciously. – Everything you read was true, as it goes; there wasn't much room for exaggeration. I disguised myself as a man and joined the army. I found it very hard at first, then I got to like it. I was careful; and if I hadn't told, no one would have ever found out. I met Bill at a shooting match. He was so handsome I just fell for him straight away, and told him how I was.

She paused.

– In a really dumb moment we got married. We were on leave at the same time so I borrowed some clothes and we went to a town hall. It was spring and all the fruit trees were in blossom. Strangers were our witnesses; they thought us a very romantic pair. When we went back it was all right at first and then things changed.

– He told the commanding officer about me, so I'd have to leave. He never denied it was him, said it was for my own sake. I said all sorts of foolish things about how he couldn't love me any more. He didn't bother to contradict. When I said he'd cut me off from my whole life, he just laughed and walked away. I was so mad, I just took the gun he'd given me, called his name to make him turn, and shot him in the hand.

– The first two fingers of his right hand, said Jenny.

– That's how I aimed. So he'd have to leave as well.

– You interest me, Phoebe Gray, said Jenny. – I think we should be friends, as well as you working for me.

– I'm working for the carnival, Phoebe corrected.

– I'll come and see your first performance.

Two

The carnival took place in and around a collection of ramshackle sheds at the edge of the town. The snow had been cleared aside, or packed down by the constant traffic of feet and carts. A makeshift paling enclosed the site; the last mark against the desolate white meadows stretching up to the mountainous horizon.

When darkness came abruptly in mid-afternoon a fire was

154

lit in the centre of the field. Children, indistinguishably wrapped, stood around, gradually peeling back their hoods as the blaze grew fierce. Various members of the circus watched, shivering, from the doors of their vans, cursing the luck that had brought them this far north at this time of the year.

Jenny Diver could see the red glow of the fire from the window of her bar. She was examining the trophies she'd brought back from her last trip, feeling a boredom she told herself was irrational. There was one necklace of rubies that excited her; she twisted them idly round beneath the light to see them shine.

When a knock came at the door she tossed the necklace into a shallow bowl already partly filled with precious stones.

– Come in.

She had recognised Moses' knock.

– I want you to meet Mr Steele, who's to be my deputy.

Her gaze passed from the old white-haired man to the tall stranger at his side.

– Mrs Diver manages the bar here.

– I hope you'll call on me if you need any help, Mrs Diver.

His voice was pleasant. She appraised his fine features, dark hair and skin. She thought him perhaps too well aware of how handsome he was.

– I'm happy to meet you, Mr Steele, she said, and held out her hand.

There was a fractional hesitation before he took it with his left. Jenny was on her guard. The pressure was firm and cool.

– I'll see you at the fair, whispered Moses in turn. Jenny felt Steele's eyes on her for a second as he left the room.

– Watch her, said Moses once they were out in the street. Steele shrugged. – Walk up to the fair with me. You'll see everyone there.

Jenny dressed herself warmly and followed them. She slipped past at the entrance to the big tent, in the sudden press.

The shadow of the flames leapt against the canvas wall. Jenny paced carefully round the back, trying to stop her own shadow falling on its pale surface. She listened for the sound of gunfire, then passed into a small shed where Phoebe's yellow head and straight back were poised tense as her hand chopped down on the gun, firing again and again.

There was a rose pattern of marks on the target at the far end.

– Very nice.

– Jenny Diver, said Phoebe. – You look different but your voice is the same.

Her face was flushed with exertion.

– Are you nervous?

– No.

Phoebe broke open the gun and squinted down it. – Would you like to volunteer for this evening?

– Do you want to get used to shooting at me?

Phoebe smiled. – I thought perhaps you could do with a little excitement.

– What a mind-reader! Do you know your husband's here?

Phoebe shrugged. – I haven't tried to hide.

– He's learning how to use his left hand.

– He needs to.

She squinted and took aim at the board again. Jenny slipped out.

She bought a plateful of cooked meat from an old woman by the fire and stood there to eat, rolling it up into little balls between her fingers.

– So your luck's still holding, Jenny.

– I'll be ready when it runs out, she said softly, staring into the flames. A fresh puff of smoke screened the figures on the far side. A slow patter of drum beats began, increasing in rapidity until a final fierce tattoo announced the opening of the show.

Moses had saved her a seat beside himself. She looked across him to the imperturbable Mr Steele, who held a recently extinguished cigar in his left hand. Moses' fingers kept straying to her knee. She took advantage of this intimacy to lean close to him.

– How did that cripple tell you he lost his hand?

She knew the allusion would please him. He managed to get his arm right round her middle and give her a good squeeze.

– Bitten by a crazy dog, he whispered.

Abruptly Steele half-turned, catching Jenny's eye across the old man's shoulder. She felt an ill-disciplined stir of attraction.

Half-hearted applause signalled the arrival of the first act. Once the lamps were extinguished, Jenny gently detached Moses' fingers from her thigh. There was a slight groan of protest but she knew he'd soon become absorbed in what he was watching.

Indifferent grumpy clowns were followed by tumblers whose muscles had been cramped by the cold. They notched up mistake after mistake while the crowd kept a tally with boos. At last one hurled his sticks into the audience and ran off. Some of the crowd vaulted the low barrier to pursue him. Moses stood up, thumping his knees excitedly. Throughout, Jenny and Steele were motionless and silent.

A desperate roll of drums didn't do much to quell the crowds. Then as the yelling got to a pitch, it was punctured by shots. One quick volley and then another from the opposite side of the tent reduced the crowd to tense confusion. Jenny sensed a movement to her right as Steele stretched his legs, putting his boots up on the back of the seat in front.

Phoebe walked into the centre of the ring. She was dressed in black, her yellow hair as sharp contrast, holding a pistol calmly in either hand. She looked like a beautiful, fatal angel. There was a chorus of wolf whistles from the at first silent crowd. She acknowledged them gravely, bowing to each side of the ring in turn. Then Jenny saw her turn and speak to someone, so the targets were brought in. There was a slight smile. She fired the rose pattern so quickly that the shots seemed to stand in the air even after she'd finished.

There was a ripple of genuine applause. To her right Jenny heard a strange sound, and saw Steele gravely clapping his hand against his leg. The ringmaster came forward and threw various objects in the air for Phoebe to shoot. But this repertoire ran out of steam. She hit everything right each time, but there was no excitement. The crowd was growing restless. Jenny saw Phoebe glance round, then say something to the ringmaster. He held up his hand.

– The lady wants a volunteer. Any man or woman old enough to know what they're doing and not too old to care.

For a moment's silence the crowd seemed to think. Then Steele unfolded his long legs and stood up.

– I would like to volunteer.

There was in interesting inflexion in his voice. Jenny saw Phoebe shake her head slightly and smile. The ringmaster seemed anxious.

– She says you're not in perfect shape, sir. She doesn't want to be blamed for any accidents.

– I'll do, said Steele lightly. – You can tell her I won't blame her for anything.

Phoebe shrugged and spun the pistol quickly in her hand. The crowd's attention was on them as Steele walked slowly down the steps and took his place against a fresh board.

Jenny heard Moses let out a long breath of excitement beside her. Phoebe took aim at Steele, then dropped her hand and twirled round to face the crowd, polishing the gun on her sleeve. Her face betrayed nothing of what Jenny thought she must be feeling. Steele's eyes followed her, then he smiled. The woman turned back and fired, with almost agonising slowness at first and then rapidly, so when he stepped away his perfect outline was peppered on the board.

Jenny saw Phoebe's lips firm as she shook her head.

– Another volunteer, cried the ringmaster. Steele remained standing where he was. The crowd seemed to stir slightly, then settle. It was looking as one towards the man and woman in the centre of the arena.

– What do you want?

Her quiet words went right through the tent. He smiled, as if uncertain for a moment, then fumbled the cigar up to his mouth with his left hand. He took a match from his pocket and held it to the end, turning in profile to her as she stepped round silently on the sawdust so the yellow head cut across the figure in Jenny's view. He was edgy, not quite so perfect. She moved deliberately, strangely polite, though Jenny thought her hand seemed still because it was shaking too fast to be seen.

The crowd's tension seemed to absorb the noise of the shot. The match flared. A thin blue line of smoke rose from the end of the cigar.

– Thank you, he said and walked slowly back to his seat.

The crowd went wild. Jenny saw Phoebe's eyes dart to his right side, where the hand was still tucked invisibly into his pocket. Then she turned and walked out.

Jenny slipped away from Moses as they left and made her way quietly round to Phoebe's hut with the intention of witnessing an interesting scene. She had been waiting a few minutes when Steele appeared.

– Phoebe, he said quietly and knocked on the door.

Once he was inside Jenny slipped round and put her ear to it. There was nothing at first, then Steele's voice raised.

– I'll teach you to like shooting at me. I'll volunteer every day you're on. You won't be able to get anyone else. And if you leave, I'll follow you.

Jenny stepped back as he came out. The glow of the cigar revealed beads of sweat on his forehead. He paused for a moment, as if uncertain what to do, then strode off.

Three

Jenny did not allow herself to speculate on how long it would be before Phoebe came to see her. She just waited.

There were several possible developments that interested her. She kept herself calm and steady, trusting her nerves to let her make the best decisions as they became necessary.

She was serving drinks on the second night when Phoebe came in. She was pale and looked sick. Jenny poured her half a glass of whisky and watched her take her seat at a corner table.

When the bar closed she was still there. Jenny locked the door, and going over to her, shook her gently.

– I'll make some coffee.

Phoebe raised her head. – I didn't hit him tonight, she said – but one day I will. It's his hand. Every time I see him, I have to imagine what it looks like now.

Jenny's face was impassive. Then she sat down opposite Phoebe and began to communicate the details of the planned hold-up.

The next morning found her at the court-house. Before it was beginning to be light she knocked very softly at the door.

Steele opened it. – What is it?

Once inside she unwound the long black scarf she had used to disguise her appearance in the street.

– I want to see you and Moses. I need your help.

He led her through to the kitchen where they were having breakfast.

– Jenny Diver, said Moses – Have you come to give yourself up?

He pulled out a chair for her and poured her a cup of coffee.

– She says she needs help, said Steele, who lingered by the door.

Jenny sipped her coffee, eyes deliberately downcast as she felt Moses study her. At last she said

– I think someone may try to rob me this afternoon.

Moses and Steele exchanged a glance. It didn't matter that they wouldn't believe her. Their presence, if only out of curiosity, would be an important stake on her side.

She went home and spent the morning polishing glasses. Then she cleaned the mirror behind the bar, rubbing it patiently with a soft cloth until it reflected with a deep brilliance.

Opening time came too quickly. As she watched the lights flicker on across the street she felt a faint stirring of dismay, the apprehension that maybe her luck was running out at last.

Two miners came in and she served them drinks. Then Steele and Moses turned up, changing the atmosphere. Jenny found she couldn't even smile, so anxiously were her ears straining for a light footfall on the step outside.

Then she caught Steele's eye, just for a flicker. The door opened and Phoebe walked in. Steele's face registered alarm, incomprehension, but Phoebe didn't seem to see him. She walked straight on towards Jenny herself and Jenny felt her hands go up in a response that was not merely play-acting as the muzzle of the gun came into view.

– Phoebe, said Steele.

A look of terror came over her face. She fired at Jenny's head. As the mirror collapsed in a shower of glass, she turned and ran. Jenny, stunned but unhurt, picked herself up to find Moses fussing over her. There was a roar from the street outside.

– What's happening?

Moses supported her to the door. As she gazed out it seemed that every house was lit, every doorway spilling yellow light onto the snow over the heads of people who stood silently watching.

Phoebe was standing with her back against a truck some way up. She seemed to sag slightly, holding the gun with both hands in front of her as if it was some final barrier against harm.

– Put the gun down, said Steele.

She shook her head. – Don't come near me.

He emerged out of the shadows with his own gun in his left hand. He walked to within ten paces of her, and stood still, the gun pointing at the ground.

– Phoebe.

His voice was urgent, even emotional. – I don't aim so well with my left hand. If I shoot at you I'll probably kill you.

She sighed.

– Show me your hand, Bill. The thought of it's been haunting me these past few months.

He hesitated then raised it, a black, silk claw against the yellow light. Before he realised it she had turned the gun on herself. There was a muffled shot, and the spectators gathered round to look at the drops of blood on the snow.